ROYALS

Shifter Royalty Trilogy Book 1

S. DALAMBAKIS

COPYRIGHT

To Ashley Keller, for your non-stop encouragement, endless music inspiration, and being my very own personal cheerleader. I love you more than you know. Thank you for being just as excited about this book as I am.

To Stacey B., for giving me the courage to change my book when I was almost done. Thank you for listening to me ramble, and for letting me bounce ideas off you.

To my husband, AJ, for all the love and support, for encouraging me to follow my dreams. I love you.

PROLOGUE

200 years ago

A handmaiden runs through the halls of a stone castle, her blue dress billowing out around her. She comes to a stop in front of the queen's quarters, a royal guard blocking her path.

"Please, this is urgent. I need to speak with the queen. The prophetess has had a vision."

The guard moves allowing the handmaiden through. She is met with the steely gaze of the queen's four mates, blocking her path to the queen. They relax slightly when they see it's the queen's royal handmaiden. The queen's mates shift to the side.

"Bridgett is everything alright?" the queen asks frantically.

"No, my queen. The prophetess has had a vision."

"What is so urgent about this vision?"

"She has foreseen the demise of you and your mates. The shifter world tilting on its axis. Magic will slowly fade away. The shifter race eventually dying out. There will be two great wars. The one to come and one many years from now. One to restore what is lost, should she succeed."

One of the queen's mates goes and barricades the door.

"Did the prophetess say who?"

"She did not see the hand from which you will die. Only that is it someone close to you. That many years from now a descendant will rise and claim her true pairing. She and her four mates will lead a war and restore balance once more. She said you need to protect the future."

There was a loud boom, rattling the walls of the castle. It has begun. The queen quickly moves to a room off to the right. In the middle of the room sat a white, wooden bassinet. Rushing over, she quickly reaches in and picks up the bundle, cradling the baby to her chest. Running back into the previous room, she meets the eyes of her mates. She knows what needs to be done. The queen grabs a sack of coins from a nearby table and quickly moves to the handmaiden's side.

"Bridgett, I need you to take her. You will go through that room." She points to the left. "There is a secret passage behind the bookcase. Push on the top edge and it will open. Take the princess and run. Guard her with your life, and trust no one."

"My queen, why do you not take the passage yourself? You should go."

"I cannot. I need to stay here and stall for as long as possible." The queen kisses the baby's forehead. "I love you. I will always love you."

The queen places the baby in the handmaiden's arms. She then quickly takes the necklace from around her neck and places it around the baby's. She hands the handmaiden the coin sack, which she puts in the pocket of her dress. The castle is rocked with another hit. You can hear the stone walls crumbling. The queen's mates each quickly kiss the baby on the top of her head. You can hear fighting outside the door.

"Go, now. Tell her of me, of us. Let her know who she is." The hand-maiden nods as there is a loud boom against the door. "Run. Don't stop. Don't look back. Leave the city. Leave the country."

The handmaiden takes off to the door on the left. The door the queen had indicated. She runs straight to the bookcase, pushing on the top edge. There is a pop sound, the bookcase moves just an inch. Gripping the side, she pulls the hidden door open, just wide enough for her and the princess to squeeze through. The handmaiden peers in but the passage is too dark. Quickly, she grabs a lantern from the table, using it to light her way. As she enters the passage, she can hear someone trying to break the door down. Looking behind her, she sees there is a handle.

Placing the lantern at her feet, she grabs the handle and quickly closes the door. Thus, sealing her and the princess from the dangers about to happen. The handmaiden picks up the lantern and does what the queen wishes. She runs. The passage seems to be never-ending, with twists and turns, until she comes upon what she thinks is a dead end. But the light of the lantern shines off a handle. Placing the lantern on the ground, the handmaiden pushes on the door. Fresh air hits her face. Grabbing the lantern, the handmaiden, and the baby squeeze through the opening, closing the door behind her.

A quick look around, and she realizes she came out on the complete other side of the castle. The marina. This is why the queen told her to take the passage. The queen gave her coins as well. She was told to leave the country.

Moving as quickly as she dared, as to not draw attention to herself, she made her way to the first ship. The handmaiden spots a crew member carrying cargo onto the ship.

"Excuse me, do you know where I could find the Captain?"

"Aye, on the dock, right over there." He points to a man a few feet from where they stood.

"Thank you."

The handmaiden starts to move toward the Captain. The moonlight catches on the baby's necklace, the symbol of the Alpha Queen, a silver pendant with a star in the center and a symbol for each of the elements surrounding it. She puts the lantern down, tucking the necklace into the blanket the baby is wrapped in, before making her way to the Captain.

"Excuse me, Captain."

"Aye, Lass. What do ye want?"

"Where is your ship headed?"

"The Americas. Why?"

The handmaiden reaches into her pocket and pulls out the coin sack, "I was hoping I could buy passage. I have coin." She lifts and rattles the coins in the sack. The Captain runs a hand over his scraggly beard, contemplating.

"Is it just ye two?"

"Yes, Captain."

"Aye. Four gold coins and I'll let ye on my ship."

Giving the Captain what he wants, the handmaiden makes her way onto the ship. Before she can get settled, the crew starts to rush around. The Captain starts shouting orders. She hears one of the crew as they pass. The castle is under attack, an uprising.

The handmaiden cradles the baby closer to her chest. In no time, the ship has set sail. She watches the castle get smaller, as it burns and crumbles to the ground.

The queen and her mates were defeated.

The heir to the throne, cradled in her arm, the handmaiden weeps. A throne that will no longer exist. An heir to nothing.

CHAPTER ONE

Callyn- Present Day

I get to start my senior year at a new school, in the Podunk town of Camden Falls, Colorado. A town in the middle of nowhere. We are surrounded by mountains and forest. I'm not even sure how my father found this place. But today is the first day of school at Camden Falls High, home of the Camden Kings. It's my first day of senior year. I'm almost done just one more year. I can't wait. I can forget all about this school, these people, and this life. I can start over, be someone else, be myself. I make sure I stay invisible at school, so people don't question.

This new school will be no different. Being the new girl should make that easy. My home life is not all sunshine and apple pie. I'll be eighteen soon, six months and two days to be exact, but who's counting. I just keep telling myself, just make it to eighteen. After that first hurdle, I need to hang on until graduation in May. Then I'm gone, never looking back, never coming back.

It's the first day of senior year. I should be worrying about having a boyfriend or friends. What parties I'm going to on the weekends, my hair, makeup, and what I'm wearing to homecoming and prom. Instead, I'm checking to make sure my shirt sleeves are long enough to hide the bruises on my arms and long enough to hide the welts and bruising on my back, should my shirt ever rise. I keep my long, red hair straight and down to hide my face. I'm afraid people will guess or see what is wrong. I can't let them find out. It will only make things worse.

Have I thought about calling the police? Of course, but the fear I have has overridden any logical thinking. So, I suffer, for now.

I choose a black plaid, three-quarter sleeve, button-up shirt. I put a black cami on underneath, a pair of faded out blue jeans, and my black ankle boots. I don't bother with makeup because the one and only time I decided to wear it is still etched in my mind. The way my father back-handed me across my face, calling me a whore, telling me I was asking for attention from the perverted boys at school. He followed that up with a belt across my back. That was the only time he touched my face. Those are the bruises that you can't hide. Makeup can only do so much, but I can't wear it. I learned over the years how to avoid him. Sometimes though, I still can't.

When he drinks, the beatings and hitting are worse. He was never like this before my mother died. He changed that day, and not for the better. I shake my head and take a couple of deep breaths and try to shove those memories away. I grab my bookbag and walk the six blocks to school. I could ride the bus, but then I would have to share a seat with someone, and I can't have that. I like walking anyway. It's good exercise, and the fresh air always helps clear my mind and gets me in the right headspace.

My classes this year are college prep courses. My last school didn't have that option. If I take them now, then I don't have to take them in college. I'm hoping to get a full academic scholarship, and I should with my G.P.A. I make a quick stop at my locker, leaving my bookbag, and only grabbing a couple of notebooks and pens. I head to chemistry, my first class. I always pick the same seat, middle near a window. I figure the seat is inconspicuous. Sitting down, I open my notebook, looking up at the right time to watch two of the hottest guys I have ever seen walk in.

They look quickly around the room and head in my direction. They take up the table in front of me. The classroom is set up like a lab. The tables are long enough to seat three people at each. There are drawers that house the chemistry equipment. In the back, in locked cabinets, are chemicals. The chairs are wooden stools. I keep my head down and peek up at them.

They are gorgeous. The one in the middle seat, his light brown hair is faded on the sides and long on top. His eyes, oh his eyes. They are like a gold hazel color. He has broad shoulders and toned arms. He looks good in his green t-shirt and blue jeans. His friend, on the other hand, has copper, wavy hair, just long enough to run your fingers through it. He has nice deep brown eyes. His build is similar to his friends, not as bulky, but still has some muscle tone. Even his blue t-shirt can't hide that. They talk amongst themselves, briefly glancing back once. I feel drawn to them. I don't understand why. As much as I would like to talk to them, or anyone, I know it's for the best that I don't. I'm not sure I would even know what to say, or if they would even talk to me. My chemistry teacher comes in, breaking through my thoughts.

He is younger than I would have thought for a chemistry teacher. I would guess he is in his forties. He is wearing black, shiny shoes, and blue jeans, a white button-up shirt and a navy blue, blazer jacket. There is a lot of gel in his blonde hair. It's styled so meticulously, not a hair out of place. His brown eyes look kind. He does have a sharp jawline and a strong prominent nose. Overall, he is good looking. He sets his well-worn briefcase down on his desk.

"Good morning, everyone."

Good morning rumbles from the class. Chemistry is not the best subject to have first thing in the morning.

"I'm Mr. Calloway and welcome to Chemistry. The majority of the work will be done in groups, which I am assigning." A collective groan is heard throughout the class. "Yes, yes, I know, but this is to ensure that work will be done. Now when I call your names, move to a table with your partners. This is how you should sit for the remainder of the semester."

Mr. Calloway starts calling out names and the sounds of shuffling and murmurs can be heard. I sit patiently waiting for him to call my name. I'm going to have to talk to people. I start to panic. It will only be for this class. I can do this. I can do this. Then it happens.

"Callyn Silvers, Zeke Montgomery, and Lucian Harris."

I glance around the room trying to figure out who they are, when I spot the two good-looking boys in front of me, also looking around the room trying to figure out who I am. I grab my notebooks and pens and move to the only seat left at their table. The spot next to the brown-haired boy. They both look at me with curious interest.

"Hi, I'm Callyn."

"Zeke."

"Lucian." My fellow ginger.

I smile shyly and duck my head. The teacher goes on explaining what is expected of us for the semester and hands out our books. By the time he is done, the bell rings. I gather my stuff and look over to the guys.

"See you tomorrow," I say quickly, then leave.

As I walk to my next class, I think about chemistry. I really said something to them and the world didn't crash and burn. Maybe I can have a friend. Friends that I would only see at school. Maybe, but I need to slow down. I need to get comfortable talking to people first and chemistry is just my way to do it.

CHAPTER TWO

The Boys-Zeke

"Man, can you believe it's senior year," I say as I shove at Lucian's shoulder. He shoves me back.

"Hey man, enjoy it. Next comes college and going out into the real world."

"Yeah, but I'm tired of all the drama that comes with high school. It's the same shit different year."

"I get it, but I still want to enjoy this."

I see Maximus, or Max as we call him, and Graydon walking down the hall towards us. I lean on the locker next to Lucians. "We will."

"Where is everyone's first class? I have Trig." Max asks.

"Me and Lucian have Chemistry," I answer.

"English," Graydon grumbles.

We all chuckle. English is Graydon's least favorite subject and add-on that it's his first class in the morning. I shake my head and laugh. We talk for a couple more minutes about our schedules and agree to meet up for lunch before heading off to our classes. Upon entering the class, me and Lucian take a quick look around the room. There are only two tables left with two open spots. A girl with red hair is sitting alone at one, and the table in front of her is empty. As we make our way over, the most incredible scent hits my nose, vanilla, and strawberries.

Mine.

Whoa. Where did that thought come from? We sit at the table in front of her, and that's when I notice the smell is her. I can feel my teeth lengthen. The urge to mark her is strong. Then it hits me, she's my mate. I found my mate. I don't even know this girl. I have to distract myself until I can talk to the guys. I take a small inhale, trying to scent what kind of shifter she is, but I don't scent one. Fuck, she's human. How is a human, my mate? That shouldn't be possible. I'm going to have talk to the Elder Council.

Lucian grabs my attention. "So, there is a new girl."

We both glance behind us. Damn, she's beautiful. And she's mine. Luckily, the teacher walks in, drawing my attention to him. He says he is going to assign partners. I roll my eyes. The rest of the class isn't too happy about it, but what are you going to do? I wait for my name to be called and hope I'm paired with someone who will do work. Hopefully, I can get paired with the new girl.

"Callyn Silvers, Zeke Montgomery, and Lucian Harris," the teacher calls.

Hell yeah, I got Lucian. I don't recognize the girl's name. I look around the room. Next thing I know the girl who is sitting behind us moves and sits next to me. I barely hold back a groan. I take a deep breath, drawing in her scent. My wolf wants to brush up against her and coat his fur in her scent.

"Hi, I'm Callyn," she says.

"Zeke," I manage to say. I'm surprised, to say the least. Her face is free of makeup. There is a splattering of freckles across the bridge of her nose and cheeks. Her eyes are a light brown with gold flecks. Her voice, oh man, it's soft but slightly raspy. It's the sexiest thing I've heard. I hear Lucian say his name. The teacher pulls her attention.

She is beautiful. I keep looking at her. I just want to get to know her, touch her, claim her. Before I know it, class is over. She gathers her things.

"See you tomorrow," she says with a smile and leaves.

That smile, holy shit. Thank God, I'm sitting. I stare at her hips as she walks away. Good lord. Lucian taps me on the shoulder. I see it on his face too. This girl is about to turn our lives upside down.

Lucian

I tap Zeke on the shoulder. We need to get going or we'll be late for our next classes. When he looks at me, I see the sucker punched look on his face. I know because I have the same expression on my face. I wouldn't have believed anyone if they told me. But I found her. I really found her.

My mate.

And she is the most beautiful girl I have ever laid eyes on. We grab our stuff and haul ass. I make it to my class right before the bell rings. Sitting in the first available seat, I pull my phone out and hide it under the desk as I send a message to Zeke.

Me: Damn, chem is going to be interesting.

Zeke: Yeah. I need to tell you something, but I want to wait until lunch when Graydon and Max will be there. I want to tell everyone at the same time.

Me: Everything ok?

Zeke: Yeah, just something important happened. If I'm honest, I still don't believe it.

Me: That works, because I need to tell everyone something too.

Me: I don't know what to do about it.

Zeke: Is it serious? You know we will all be there for you.

Me: I know. It is life changing.

Zeke: Same here.

Well, shit. I wonder what his could be? I'm going to have to talk to my grandfather about this. As far as I know, no human has ever been mated to a shifter. Let alone, that human being a destined mate. Destined mates are few and far in between. They are the one being put on this planet, that is made for you. They are the other half of your soul. Destined mates mean everything to a shifter. Now, more so than ever. Fewer shifters every year are able to find their destined mates. Eventually, shifters will cease to exist, because of some war that happened 200 years ago. That war ended the life of the Alpha Queen and her mates. In the process, ending the last true alpha mate pairing.

True alpha mate pairings helped stabilize the magic that makes shifters possible. It is said that the Alpha Queen, with the help of her mates, helped harness the magic. I'm not quite sure how that works, yet. My grandfather has yet to teach me this. But now, with me having a human destined mate, he can't put this off any longer. I found her. I need to know.

I put my phone away and try to pay attention, but I can't. My mind keeps wandering back to Callyn. That is how I spend my next couple of classes. Lunch couldn't come fast enough. I grab my lunch and sit next to Zeke. Max and Graydon are sitting across from me.

"So, there's this cute redhead in my English class. We got paired up to work on our first project," Max says as I sit.

"There was this cute red head in my math class that got called on to work this problem out on the board," Graydon says.

I look over at Zeke. It couldn't be the same redhead. "Me and Zeke are paired with a cute redhead in Chemistry."

"Huh," Max exclaims. "Petite, long red hair, brown eyes, freckles, new?"

All of us nod. I swear it's as if we somehow manifested her because there she is walking by our table. We all follow her as she takes a seat at an empty table.

Mine.

The urge to go to her is overwhelming.

Zeke clears his throat, grabbing our attention. "About her. She's my mate."

What? How? That can't be right. Am I wrong? No. I've been told you would know, and I've never had this feeling before.

"You're not going to like hearing this, but she's my mate."

Graydon

What the hell is going on here? Zeke says she's his mate. Then

Lucian. But they're wrong. They must be because she is my mate. I knew the moment I caught a whiff of her scent. The smell is intoxicating.

"Hate to burst your bubbles, but she is mine. My mate."

"No, all of you have it wrong because she is my mate," Max chimes in.

Now, the whole table is glaring at each other. There's no way she can be the mate to all four of us. So, three of us have it wrong and it's not me. Her scent called to my bear. The lazy fool perked right up the moment the vanilla and strawberry scent hit his nose. Now, he is lumbering back and forth telling me to go and take what is ours. Can't say I disagree with him but now we need to sort this mess out.

Lucian sighs, "Looks like a trip to the Elder Council is in store for us. Maybe my grandfather will know what is happening."

Lucian's grandfather is a member of the Elder Council. Lucian is being groomed to take his spot once he is old enough and his grandfather is ready to retire. Glad it's not me. It's a shit job, but that's just my opinion. It's really a position of prestige and honor. Yeah, fuck that.

"No sense in arguing about it now. Side note, since she's new that means she has no friends. I say we fix that and be the first." Max says with a Cheshire grin.

I know what he is doing, and I can't fault his logic. He wants us to stake our claim. I was up and out of my seat in a heartbeat. No way was I going to sit here and let my mate sit by herself. I am at her table in a couple of strides.

"Do you want some company?" I ask as I sit down taking the seat across from her. I'm not really giving her a choice. I'm trying to be polite. Her eyes widen in surprise when she looks up. I saw her earlier, but nothing beats sitting this close. I get to really see her. Her eyes are a light brown, like a rich honey color. And we all know how bears love their honey. I could get lost in her eyes. Her creamy pale skin is dusted with freckles. Her red hair almost reaches the top of her butt. I could drink my fill of her, and it would never be enough.

"You don't have to. I'm fine being on my own." Her voice grabbing my attention. The raspiness is the sexiest thing I've heard.

"I know I don't have to; I want to." She smiles at me and it could very well be my undoing. I smile back. The rest of the guys quickly follow.

Max took her right side, Lucian her left, and Zeke sitting next to me. "I'm Graydon James. You know Zeke Montgomery, Lucian Harris, and Maximus Anderson, or Max to us."

"What are you guys doing? Is this some kind of prank? I really don't need to be the butt of a joke. Did you come over here to pick on the new girl?" she questions.

"No, Callyn. This is not a joke. We didn't come over here to pick on you either. We all want to be your friends," Lucian says and gives her arm a gentle squeeze.

She winces. My eyes narrow. Did Lucian squeeze her arm too hard? I swear if he did, I'm going to beat his ass. I don't care who you are, no one hurts my mate.

"Why? What makes me so special?"

Well, shit. I don't know how to answer this. I want to tell her the truth, but chances are she would think I'm crazy. I doubt she would believe me anyway. Lucian on the other hand is usually pretty good in these kinds of situations.

"We would like a chance to get to know you and we hope you'll want to get to know us. You're partnered with most of us in some of your classes. We're going to be spending a lot of time together. It can't hurt to make friends with the people you are going to be interacting with on a daily basis." Lucian states.

"I don't know. The hottest guys at school all want to be my friend. It sounds fishy."

"So, you think we're the hottest guys in school, huh?" Max asked as he gently bumps her shoulder.

Callyn rolls her eyes, flinching slightly. If that isn't the cutest thing. Man, this girl is already making me soft. I just thought something was cute. I'm gonna lose my man card if I ever say this shit out loud.

"You know you are. Plus, some girls have been giving me the side eye since the four of you sat down. You all must be a big deal here."

You could say that, but I only have eyes for one girl. The one sitting right across from me.

Maximus

Ha. She thinks we're good looking. She's not wrong. All the girls that go to school here have tried to get our attention. Don't get me wrong, the girls are pretty, but some have some ugly insides. The way things were going, I would have ended up with one of them, because of how hard it is to find your destined mate. Thank whatever forces brought Callyn to me.

As I look to my friends, I can see that they are all enamored with her as well. I know even if she wasn't my mate, I would still be interested. But the fact that she is makes it all the sweeter. The bell rings and we get up to throw our stuff away. Callyn tries to sneak away, but I grab her hand.

"And just where do you think you're going? Are you trying to give us the slip?"

"I'm trying to head to class."

"Which are...," I trail off.

"Art, gym, and study hall."

"Good, I have art," Zeke says.

"So, do I," Graydon claims.

"We all have study hall," I say.

She nods. "See you in study hall then?" she questions.

"Definitely."

I reluctantly let go of her hand. I watch as Zeke and Graydon flank her sides and walk down the hall. I look over at Lucian and see he is staring too.

"We gotta get going or we'll be late, and I was almost late once today," Lucian says.

We head in opposite directions and I think about Callyn the whole time. I saw the wince she gave when Lucian squeezed her arm. He didn't squeeze that hard. There is no way that should have hurt. If I noticed, then I know the others saw it as well. Eventually, we'll find out. I make it to class just as the late bell rings. I take the only available seat which is in the front. I can't concentrate. I can't even pull out my phone. Sitting up front sucks. Focus Max. I laugh to myself. No way that is happening. I just give in and let my mind wander to Callyn.

I can't wait to learn more about her. The little bit of time I've spent with her today, you can tell she's different. In a good way. I was a little hurt that she questioned why we would want to be friends with her. I wonder what happened to make her think that. I guess it doesn't help being the new kid. Makes me wonder if she was picked on in her other school. Well, that is about to change. Callyn doesn't know what's coming her way with the four of us in her life now.

CHAPTER THREE

Callyn

I didn't have much time to think about what this could mean for me having four big, muscular, good-looking guys as friends. Zeke and Graydon kept me occupied during art. They make it hard to concentrate. I already checked Zeke out during chemistry, but Graydon is no less hot. His inky, black hair is long and thick on top and faded on the sides. I have the strangest urge to run my fingers through it. His eyes are green, like moss. He must not have shaved yesterday because he has the shadow of stubble on his face. It only serves to increase his hotness. Muscle wise he is almost as big as Zeke.

Graydon can fill out a pair of jeans. I may have looked once or twice. His biker boots were working for me. Ugh. Having them around is going to be hard because I can't stop looking at them. They are good looking individually, but together...together the view is stunning. Even Maximus. He has your boy next door look. Blonde hair and blue eyes. His hair is long and reaches the top of his shoulders. He's smaller than Zeke and Graydon, but you can tell there is some muscle tone to him. At my old schools, I was never really into any of the boys. But these four are a different story. I feel this unusual pull toward them. I want to be near them. Their presence is calming. I don't know what to think about that.

While we were in art class, they told me about themselves and asked me questions, which I tried to deflect. I don't have a lot of good memories and I don't do anything. I hide in my room and study and try not to be around my father. I keep hoping that one day he will forget that I am there, but no such luck.

I'm out of here when I graduate. I won't be coming back. The way that my father treats me, I'm glad I don't have any siblings. I can only imagine what he could be doing to them. I shake my head. I digress. As much as I tried to keep changing the topic from me back to one of them, they wouldn't let me. So, I gave them answers, but they were vague. I got a little break from them in gym class. Luckily, none of them were in it. Gym kept my mind occupied as well. No time to think about them while you are too busy trying not to fall over your own two feet. Athletically gifted I am not.

I make my way to study hall. The boys are already there. There is a seat open between Maximus and Graydon. Lucian is in the seat in front of Graydon, and Zeke is in front of Max.

"There she is," Max says. "We saved you a seat." He does a gesture with his hand toward the empty seat that reminds me of the models on the Price is Right.

I smirk and shake my head, making my way over and sitting in the open seat. I look at Max, he has this impish smile on his face. Oh, he is going to be trouble, or get me into trouble. I sneak a peek at Graydon. He seems to have a permanent scowl on his face. I just want to reach over and smooth the wrinkles that form between his eyebrows. I look away before I do. I don't think he would appreciate my hands on him.

Instead, I take out my books and start working on math homework. I know, I know, it's the first day and we already have homework. Well, at least I have an hour before the end of school to start it. I can hear the boys around me making plans for the weekend. I ignore it and continue working. A little while later I feel a tap on my shoulder and almost jump out of my seat. I turn around. It was Graydon. I take a deep breath and try to calm my rapidly beating heart.

"Sorry, I didn't mean to scare you," Graydon says sheepishly.

"It's okay." No way was I telling him that I thought my father was trying to touch me. I forgot where I was. It is kind of alarming. I'm always on guard because I never know what can happen on a day to day basis. I feel comfortable around them, safe. I don't know how. I just met them.

"What are you doing this weekend?" Graydon's question breaks my train of thought.

"Oh, um. Nothing."

"Really? Do you want to hang out with us? There is a party out at the Michaelson's Saturday night."

"I can't. Plus, partying isn't really my thing."

"We'll make sure you have fun. I promise nothing bad will happen. We'll be your own personal bodyguards."

"I don't know. I'll think about it and let you know."

"Do you have a cell phone, so we can all exchange numbers? That way if you change your mind you can get a hold of us."

"Yeah." It's the one thing I have kept a secret from my father. He doesn't know about it. I make sure the bills are paid. It's the only way I can have it. I pull my phone out of my pocket. It takes a couple of minutes, but we all exchange numbers. Their numbers are the only ones in there. I honestly don't know why I have the phone. I never call or text anyone. I guess I like the security it gives me, in case I ever need to use it.

The bell rings. We all gather our things and head to our lockers. Max and Graydon are first. I keep walking, but a tug on my hand stops me.

"Where do you think you're going?" Zeke asks.

"Trying to slip away again? That's twice in one day. You're starting to hurt my feelings." Maximus gives me this puppy dog look and pouts his lips. He pushes his hair behind his ears.

The look is pathetic, but it does make me feel guilty. That is exactly what I am trying to do. "I was just going to my locker."

"Just wait. We'll all go together to everyone's lockers."

"Why? Doesn't it make more sense if everyone goes to their own lockers, get their stuff, and then meet outside?"

"Yeah, probably, but we have always done it this way."

I roll my eyes. I really don't have time for this. I have to walk home. I need to beat my father. Surprisingly, he functions enough during the day to keep a job, but the second that he gets home, he starts drinking.

"Do you have to catch the bus home?" Zeke questions.

"No, I just have to get home." Max and Graydon close their lockers and we walk to Lucian's and then Zeke's. Of course, mine would be the one closest to the front door and therefore last. Ugh.

"We can give you a ride home," Graydon offers.

"NO." I clear my throat. "No, that's okay, I can walk. Thank you for the offer though."

I look at Graydon and see him sharing a look with the others. After Lucian and Zeke are done getting their things, we walk to my locker. I quickly grab my bookbag and shove in all my books and notebooks. I carefully put the straps over my shoulders. Even with the bookbag lying flat against my back, it hurts like hell. The bruises are only three days old. They're still sore. The walk home is going to be torture. I turn to look at the guys and see that they are all staring at me. Did they see how I eased my bookbag on my shoulders? If they did, no one mentions anything.

I follow them out to the parking lot. They stop by a black truck.

"You all ride to school together too? Is there anything that you do by yourselves? How exactly does that work when Zeke has football practice?" Seriously Callyn. Shut up. Since when do you open your mouth about anything? You don't know these boys. You don't know what they're capable of. You have been doing this all day and you need to stop.

But one of the things that Zeke mentioned about himself in art class, was that he played football. He is a defensive end. I'm not sure what that means since I'm not that into sports, but he seemed excited about it. Graydon told me he liked motorcycles and sometimes picked up a shift at the local bike shop. He says he mostly helps clean up, but he is hoping that one day he can become an apprentice to learn to build them from the ground up.

I shake my head. "I'm sorry. I shouldn't have said that it was rude."

"No worries," Zeke says with a wink. "But yes, we all ride to school together. We don't live that far from each other. We just take turns on who is driving in the morning when none of us have to stay after school. Though usually, they don't mind waiting. Since today is the first day of school, coach gave us the day off."

It must be nice having such close friendships. Maybe one day we can have that too. "I'll see you guys tomorrow." I start to walk away.

"Are you sure we can't give you a ride home? There is plenty of room."

I wave my hand above my head. "I'll be fine, but thanks." I walk the six blocks home.

♛ ♛ ♛ ♛ ♛

I put my bookbag on the kitchen chair. I look through the cupboards to see what I could make for dinner. Spaghetti and meatballs sound good. I check the freezer to see if we have frozen meatballs. We do. Oooh, garlic bread!

Gathering the ingredients, I start making dinner. No sooner than I put the water on the stove, my phone vibrates. I look to see that not one, but all the boys have texted me to see if I made it home okay. I couldn't help but smile as I reply.

CHAPTER FOUR

The Boys- Graydon

"I don't like that she is walking home. None of us know how far away she lives. It doesn't feel right. I'm not just talking about her walking home by herself either. Something is going on at home. She practically bit my head off when I offered to give her a ride. It's like she doesn't want us to know where she lives," I say as we all get in my car.

I make my way over to Zeke's house and pull into his driveway. I wasn't kidding when I said we all live close. We all live on the same street, Zeke at one end, me at the other. Lucian lives across the street from me and Max a couple of houses down from him. We grew up together and have been friends since we were kids. None of us make a move to get out of the car.

"How long do you think we should give her to get home?" Lucian asks.

"I don't know. 20 minutes. We don't know where she lives. It can't be too far if she walks home," Max answers.

Exactly 20 minutes later we all text her.

Me: Hey, just checking to see if you made it home okay.

Callyn: Yes, I did thank you for asking. :)

Callyn: You know the others texted me too...lol

Me: Yeah, we're all still sitting in my car. None of us liked the idea of you walking home.

Callyn: Why are you all still in your car? I know, but I've been walking home for years. I've walked home at all my other schools.

Me: Yeah, we were waiting for you to text one of us back. I get it, but I still don't have to like the idea. Maybe you'll let us give you a ride home tomorrow?

Callyn: Not likely...lol. There are just some things I'm not ready to share yet. I mean we just became friends. I need to get to know you, all of you guys.

Me: I understand. We won't pressure you. That doesn't mean we won't ask every day.

Callyn: Thank you. That means a lot to me. Who knows, maybe one day I'll say yes. See you tomorrow.

Me: See you tomorrow.

I look around and see I'm the only one who is still texting her. All of them are giving me a weird look.

"What?" I say with more venom than necessary. I don't like the looks they are giving me. It's not my fault that she was messaging me. They can't get mad at me for it.

"What did she say?" Lucian questions.

"She got home safe. I asked her if she would let us give her a ride home tomorrow. She said not likely, that there are some things that she is not ready to share with us yet." Zeke's eyebrows scrunched together.

"I knew something was going on. Did you see her face when Lucian touched her arm earlier?" Zeke states.

"I also saw her flinch when Max bumped shoulders with her. You know she isn't going to tell us shit," I stated angrily.

"Not yet. We have to get her to trust us," Lucian says.

We all nod our head in agreement. We just have to take our time, because the second we push her, she'll run away. I like her. She's my mate, I can't lose her.

"We will when the time is right, and that time is not right now. We have to gain her trust first and *she* has to be the one to tell us that something is wrong. Did anyone ever think that maybe we are all overreacting and there is nothing wrong? Maybe she is just uncomfortable around all of us, four big guys she doesn't know approached her. She has every right to be cautious. Plus, we need to trust her. She's about to be thrust into a world she has no idea even exists. We have to make sure she is ready for that," Lucian states.

He is right, it's hard not to do anything. She's my mate, I want to protect her; and I will, the second I can. When I do, I will tear the heads off anyone who harms her.

Zeke

Is she being abused? What if she is being inappropriately touched? I can't even say the right word. It's too horrible and sick to even think about. God, I hope I'm wrong on both accounts. What if I'm not? What if someone is hurting her? Don't let me find out someone is hurting her. I clench my fist. What kind of asshole does that to someone? What kind of man or woman does that make you? One of the worst kinds. I have no tolerance for those kinds of people. I growl low in my throat.

"We have to do something." My voice is barely coming out human.

"What would you like us to do?" Graydon practically yells.

"I don't know," I say frustrated. "I know we can't do anything yet, and I hate it. I hope we're wrong."

"We all do," says Max.

"How about we go inside. You know my mom has food cooking. Let's eat and do homework. Then figure out a way to get Callyn to trust us. Maybe we can ask my mom? She always gives good advice." The guys all nod their heads in agreement.

We all get out and shuffle into the house. It's just me and my mom here. We don't have a very big house, but my mom works her ass off to provide for us. I got a job to try and help, but I don't get many hours since I'm still in school and play football. If my mom had it her way I wouldn't work, but the little bit I do make pays for the gas in my truck, lunches out, and dates (which I don't really go on). I figure the less money coming out of her pocket, the better. It means more money for food and bills.

I just wish I didn't have a deadbeat father. He bailed on us the minute he found out that my mom was pregnant. Which is unusual for a shifter, but we found out he had a family somewhere else. Neither woman was his destined mate because, after the feelings that have surfaced just from today, from meeting my mate, I don't know how he could do anything that he has done. How he could intentionally hurt his mate? I would rather die. Which is also why knowing something is going on with her and I can't do anything about it, is killing me. I've heard all my life about what I could feel if I ever met my mate. It pales in comparison.

After my father left, he never contacted us. It is what it is, and my mom has plenty made up for it. My house is a small two-bedroom, two-story home. The living room is to the right, the kitchen is to the left when you walk in the front door. The laundry room is down the hall and there is a storage closet across from the laundry room. There are stairs in front of me that lead to the upstairs, where there are two bedrooms and a bathroom. We all walk into the kitchen and there is my mom making dinner. I walk over and give her a hug.

My mother is in her late thirties, but you wouldn't know it. She takes care of herself. Her brown hair is braided down her back. It's the same color as mine. Her blue eyes always seem to see right through me. She is short, only coming to my shoulders. She might be small, but I know better than to try to pull anything over on her.

"Hey, Mom. The guys are here. We're going to the dining room to work on some homework."

"It's the first day Zeke. They gave you homework already?"

"Yeah. Not much. The guys are probably going to stay for dinner. Is there enough?"

"Of course." She looks over at me. She must have seen something on my face.

"Is there something else, Zeke? Is it serious? Are you guys in some sort of trouble? Is everyone okay?"

"Yes, it's probably serious. No, we are not in trouble. Yes, everyone is fine."

"Okay. Just checking. Dinner will be done in thirty. We'll talk then."

"Thank you, Mom," I say and give her a quick kiss on the cheek. I see the smirk on her face as she swats at my arm.

"Go do your homework."

If anyone can give us some insight, it will be my mom. I just hope to hear something good.

Maximus

Zeke's mom always makes the best food. One of my favorites is her homemade tacos, which she made today. She even fries the shells and shapes them herself. "This is so good Miss M," I say as I shovel food in my mouth.

"Glad you like it, Max," she chuckles. "So, how about you guys tell me what's going on."

All of us look over to Lucian. He is better at explaining things. I try to keep everything light-hearted, the jokester if you will. Lucian tells Miss M what happened and what we suspect. She is quiet for a moment.

"Alright boys, I need you to listen and listen good. You are probably right, and something is going on at home. I pray what we are all thinking is wrong, but in case you are right, you will not pester her about this. Do you hear me?" We all nod our heads. "*She* has to be one to tell you. If you ask her about it or bug her, she won't tell you anything. You will, in fact, push her away. Now, I know you boys mean well, but you just met her. Give her some time to get to know you, and for you to know her. When she is ready, she will come to you, then you can act. This girl has no idea any of this exists, that alone will shock her. You know what she is and are half driven right now by your animals. You know what this means, she doesn't. Just take your time with her. You also need to go and talk to the Elder Council."

Miss M gets up and starts to clear the dishes. She turns back, "I believe you are all destined to be her mates. I believe that she hasn't known love in a long time, and it seems like fate is going to be making that up to her, with the four of you. I also feel like something bigger is at play. Just be careful. Talk to the Elder Council, they will be able to help you more," she says.

"What do you mean, Mom?"

"She is the mate to all of you. I'm not sure why it is happening now, but the last female to have four mates died around 200 years ago. A true alpha pairing is what it is called. Like I said it is something that you need to talk to the Elder Council about, they will have more answers." She puts the dishes in the sink and walks out of the kitchen.

"Well, shit," exclaims Graydon. We all look at each other.

"One thing at a time. Your mom is right Zeke. We must wait for her to come to us. Let's just be her friends and show her that we are not going anywhere. That will be the first step. Then hopefully with a little bit of time and patience, she will be comfortable enough with us to tell us what is going on."

"What do you think, Lucian? You've been awfully quiet," questions Graydon.

"I don't know what to say that wasn't already. I agree with everyone. When I go home, I'll ask my grandfather when we can go and speak to the Elder Council," he says as he shrugs.

I get the sense that he is leaving something out. "You sure?"

He sighs. "I don't know." He runs his hands down his face and leans back in his chair. "Look I like her. I'm not going to lie. I can't stop thinking about her. Even right now, I'm wondering what she is doing. I just want to get to know her. I want to be around her, she is beautiful. I know some of this is the fact that we are destined mates." He shrugs his shoulders. "She's not like other girls. Now, with what Zeke's mom said, there is even more uncertainty. I just hope she can handle everything. Hell, I hope we can."

He looks around to all of us. "But whatever comes my way, I will deal with. I don't care what you decide, but I'm not going to let my mate go. She is good, even with whatever she has been, and is still, going through, she is good. Can't you see it?" Lucian gets up from the table, grabs his bookbag. "She needs someone to fight for her for once, and I will. I'm going home. I'll talk to you guys later." A few seconds later the front door closes.

We are all sitting here with our mouths open. Lucian doesn't say much, well not much about his feelings. This is surprising, to say the least. I meet Zeke and Graydon's eyes.

"Well damn."

Lucian

I walk down the street to my house. I am such an idiot. I literally just told them I am going to pursue Callyn with or without them. I don't see them backing down. I know our lives just got a whole lot messier. I don't even know if she likes me. If she was a shifter I wouldn't have to question. She would feel what I do. But she's human and they don't think the same way we do. The guys are going to think I'm crazy. Hell, maybe I am. But this girl has me all twisted up inside.

I go inside the house. It's just me and my grandparents. I don't like to talk about my parents. It's still too painful. I walk to the kitchen and see a note on the table. *Luke, Went to bingo. Made dinner. Yours is in the microwave. I'll be home by 10. Grandpa had to stay late with the Council. Love, Grammy.* I smile. I love my grandmother. She has tattoos all over her arms and legs, and right now because the weather is nice, she still drives her Harley. My grandma is kind of a badass. The total opposite of my strait-laced grandfather. His gray hair always slicked back. His clothes pressed, never wrinkled. Always proper when he talks and acts. But they make it work. I leave the dinner she made in the microwave, for now, chances are I'll eat it later anyway.

I jog up the stairs and go to my bedroom. I put my bookbag down on my desk chair and plop down on my bed. I pull my phone out of my pocket and pull up Callyns name. My fingers hover over the keyboard. What do I text her? Should I text her? Would she even want to hear from me? I sigh and put the phone down next me. I glance back to the phone. Screw it. I pick the phone up and bring up Callyns name again, just text and see if she is busy. Send her a message and get to know her.

Me: Hey, you busy.

I roll my eyes. Really Lucian. You couldn't do better.

Callyn: No, just got done with dinner. How about you?

Me: Same. Just relaxing in my bedroom. Wanted to check in on you.

Callyn: :) aww Luke I'm okay, thank you for asking.

I got a smiley face and she called me Luke. I have the stupidest smirk on my face.

Me: I wanted to talk with you and get to know you. I know we just met today, but I wanted to make sure you were comfortable.

Callyn: At first you guys are kind of overwhelming, but I am comfortable around all of you, not sure why. It's strange, I'm never like this around people, especially people I just met.

Me: I understand. It's always just the four of us, but there is just something about you. Do you want to play 20 questions? I promise not to ask anything too personal. You can ask me questions as well.

Yeah. Good thinking Luke. This should be an easy way to get to know her. Since I promised not to ask anything too personal, it should be fun. She should agree, I hope. I don't have to wait too long for her reply.

Callyn: Yeah, but I get to go first.

Me: Deal

We spend the next hour just texting and sending the lame getting-to-know-you questions. Her favorite color is coral. Her favorite food is tacos. She'll have to try Miss Montgomery's tacos, she'll love them. She doesn't have a favorite sports team, because she doesn't really watch them. Well, that's going to change. I'll make a Rams fan of her yet. But it was the best conversation I've had with a girl. It was silly and stupid, and I imagine her laughing while we texted. I like everything I've learned. It makes me like her even more. I'm so screwed. There are a lot of unanswered questions, but it will work out.

It has to.

CHAPTER FIVE

Callyn

The next day at school was more of the same with the boys being overprotective. I noticed some evil glares from the girls. I never had to worry about drama before. I don't want to start now, but I have a feeling my trouble is only starting. I sigh as I walk into the house, closing and locking the door behind me. I make my way to the kitchen. I place my bookbag on one of the chairs by the kitchen table, as I make my way over to the cupboards. I open almost all of them to see what I could make for dinner.

There are instant mash potatoes and canned vegetables. I just need to see if there is some kind of meat. I check the fridge and find beef tips and gravy. The premade kind that you just pop in the microwave. That will have to do. I'm in the middle of making dinner when my phone buzzes. I pull my phone out of my pocket and lean against the counter while I check it. I see four missed texts, one from each of the boys. I couldn't stop smiling. I open each message, and they are all asking if I got home okay. It's nice that someone cares enough to check.

I'm too busy texting that I don't realize my dad pulls in the drive. We're lucky he's a functioning drunk. I've got to give myself a hand for also not ruining the food. The sound of the keys jingling in the knob grabs my attention. I panic as I frantically look for a place to put my phone. My eyes scan the countertop. Spotting the cereal container, I rush over and pop the lid tossing my phone in. I just push the container back when my father walks into the kitchen.

Crap. Crap. Crap.

I hope I left my phone on vibrate. Oh god. Why can't I remember? I hope none of them text me. My heart is beating a mile a minute. My dad narrows his eyes.

"What are you doing just standing there?"

"I-I-I was just making dinner."

I can hear a faint buzzing sound.

Shit. Please don't hear. Please don't hear. I repeat as a mantra in my head.

"Well, is it done? How about you just get the hell out of my way."

I simply nod and move to the other side, not wanting to leave the kitchen even though I should. I can't chance him finding the phone. I shudder at the thought of what he would do to me. He grunts as he makes a plate and goes to the fridge to grab a six-pack. He leaves the kitchen and goes to sit in the living room. I wait until I hear the T.V. come on before I release my breath.

I go to the container with my phone, glancing back to make sure my dad can't see me. I quickly pull my phone from the container and rush to my bookbag. Opening the front pocket and shoving my phone there. I take a deep breath, to try to calm my racing heart. That was close.

Too close.

I make a plate, grab a pop and my bookbag, and head upstairs to my bedroom. I nudge my door closed after I enter. I put my bookbag down at the foot of my bed. I move to the side and place my plate on the nightstand, before flopping back on my bed. Which hurt slightly because of the bruising. What was I thinking? I've known the guys for two days and they distract me so much that I became unaware of my surroundings. That's twice, in as many days. There is no way my father would have made it to the front door without me noticing. I hear him pulling into the drive all the time. It's how I know to try to make myself scarce.

I need to be aware of where he is at all times. It's easier to avoid him that way. Groaning as I sit up, I lean over and pull my bookbag over to me. I take my phone out and check to see who messaged me. Of course, they all do. I smile as I shake my head. These boys will be the death of me.

Lucian helped relieve some of my anxiety about meeting them when he messaged me last night. I still have some doubts about them suddenly wanting to be my friend. I can't deny that it's nice to have some for once, to not be alone. I don't even want to think about the consequences if my father found out. I shudder. I just have to be careful.

I know I won't stop being their friend. It's weird, I sort of felt connected to them from the moment we met. Drawn to them, almost like we were meant to find each other. Maybe it's because they feel safe and that isn't something that I'm used to anymore. I hope I'm right because the consequences could break me.

CHAPTER SIX

The Boys- Maximus

I thought about what Lucian said as I walked home yesterday. I'm not passing up a chance to be with my destined mate. So-what if we are all mated to her? We're all friends and this happened for a reason. I can't wait to hear what the Elder Council has to say about this. Plus, now it will be nice to have a reason to turn down the other girls at school. Don't get me wrong, the girls are pretty, and I've dated my fair share of them, but the majority of them are fake. Some of the girls here are no longer worried about finding their destined mates.

What they want is to land a guy to up their social status. For a while, they were coming after me and the others, because we each shine in a certain area. Like me, I'm good at agility. I'm fast and can outmaneuver everyone. It's helped me get out of sticky situations, a time or two. What can I say, trouble just seems to find me. Graydon excels at strength, the bear of a man. Honestly, the size of his bear is just plain overkill. Lucian can absorb information like a freaking sponge. You know it really irritates me. I have to study my ass off and all Lucian does is read it once and can remember everything. Zeke is excellent at fighting. It's like he can predetermine his opponent's next move. They never stand a chance, it's unfair really. Well, for whoever his opponent is at any rate.

The shifter females only want to be with us because of the prestige they would gain, in the shifter world that is everything. Being the best in those areas almost always guarantees you a good job in the community. The better you are, the higher up the job; the more money you make. Essentially, most shifter females are gold diggers. That is what's nice about Callyn. She has no idea about any of this and she can get to know us, for us, not for what we can give her. It would be the same with any human female. The only problem with humans is most have proven to be untrustworthy. It is why we keep our shifter sides a secret from them and don't tend to mate with any.

I wonder how Callyn will fit in with us. I smile thinking about her, which I'm pretty sure my face has been in a constant state of since yesterday. I unlock the front door and make my way to the living room.

"What's that smile for?" my mom asks.

I have a stay at home mom, one who almost always nags me about getting my haircut. I would, but I know it annoys her, so I don't. Plus, the ladies love it. My mother is tall and in her forties. She has black hair and brown eyes, but I get my coloring from my dad. My mom likes to say I'm a mini version of him. She's not wrong.

I shrug my shoulders before answering, "I met this pretty cool girl at school yesterday."

"Oh?"

I nod my head enthusiastically. "Yeah. She is new, but the best part is, she is my mate."

"Excuse me, did you just say you met your mate?"

"I did. The kicker is she is also the mate of Zeke, Lucian, and Graydon. Plus, she's human. Okay, maybe that was two kickers."

My mother is speechless for once. I chuckle. She just keeps opening and closing her mouth. Then she gives me this look. You know that mom look, the one that says I know there is more to it than this.

"Is that all?"

"No. Zeke's mom mentioned something about a true alpha pairing, but thought it was best if we all went to the Elder Council to discuss what is going on. Lucian said he would mention it to his grandfather, to see when they could see us. Also, we believe that there might be some trouble at home for her."

"I'll be damned. I have to agree with Zeke's mother. Do you want me to come with you? You boys shouldn't be dealing with any of this alone. What do you mean by trouble? Wait, did you just say she is a human?"

"The guys and me, think that Callyn, that's her name, has an abusive home life. She hasn't said anything to us, but there are signs. We don't know when we are meeting with the Council. Lucian hasn't said yet, and yeah Callyn is human."

"Are you sure? About all of this? I don't remember humans ever being able to mate with a shifter before?"

"I know. We are all just as confused by this."

She just nods her head, her eyebrows furrow. Clearly whatever she is thinking, isn't good. While my mother is distracted by her own thoughts, I leave the living room and go to my room. I debate if I should text Callyn. I really want to talk to her but at the same time, I don't want to overwhelm her. I talk myself out of it. I'll see her in the morning. Instead, I put my headphones in and lay on my bed. I browse the internet for a little bit. I need to figure out a birthday present for Lucian, seeing as how it's next week. After about an hour of looking, I give up.

Maybe I can squeeze an idea out of him tomorrow. I pull up my music app. As I am shuffling through songs, I land one that makes me think of Callyn. Before I know it, I have an entire playlist of songs that remind me of her. I groan, checking the clock on my phone. Ugh, I really should get ready for bed. I go through the motions and find myself staring at Callyn's name. I'll just send her a quick goodnight text.

Before I can chicken out, that's exactly what I do. I'm not really expecting a text back, but when my phone dings a few moments later, I can't help but get excited. My heart even picks up a few beats. The message is a simple goodnight with a smiley face emoji, but damn if I don't catch myself smiling. I plug my phone in, set the alarm, and put it on my nightstand. I close my eyes knowing that in a few short hours, I get to see her again.

Graydon

I'm grumpy as I walk down the hall. The guys are walking a few feet in front of me. God, I hate waking up early, I hate mornings, and I hate people. We had all stopped at our lockers already. Now we're on our way to Callyns. Lucky for us she is still there. They all say hi, and I'm just hanging back because I don't want to be rude. Leave it to Callyn to notice though.

"Who peed in your cornflakes this morning?"

I glare at her, not really expecting that to come out of her mouth. I just figured she was going to be shy and soft-spoken like the last two days. "No one. I just hate getting up in the mornings."

"Is that why you're not talking?"

"Yeah, I don't want to be rude."

"That would be a first," Max states. I look over and glare at him.

"Maybe you need some coffee. It should help wake you up."

I snort. "Maybe," I say with a smirk. Callyn smiles back.

"Aww, Graydon. You're just a big ole' grumpy teddy bear."

My eyes snap up to hers. She has no idea how right she is about me being a bear, but I'm definitely not a teddy bear, those ugly balls of fluff. My bear is not cute and cuddly, he's big and ferocious, like me.

She makes a move like she wants to hug me but stops. She looks up at me in shock. It's almost like she didn't expect that reaction from herself. To make sure she knew it was okay, I open my arms.

"Come on. It's okay. I promise."

Callyn hesitates. The look on her face gives away like she is having some sort of internal debate. She looks at the others, then back at me. Finally, after what seems like forever she steps into my embrace. She wraps her arms around my waist. Right before I was going to put my arms around her, I hear the softest whisper.

"Please, be easy."

I frown. "What do you mean by that?" I lightly encircle her.

She pulls back slightly. "Nothing really. I'm just sore."

"Why are you sore?" I ask as she pulls completely away.

"Oh, it's nothing." She waves a hand at me. I knew she wasn't going to answer me. I look over her shoulder to the guys, as she picks her bookbag up off the ground. They heard, and they each have a frown. Right then, the morning bell rings.

"Come on, or we're all going to be late."

Lucian, Callyn, and Zeke head down one hallway. The rest of us down another. I really hate English. I sit in my seat and take out my phone since the teacher isn't in the room yet. I pull up Lucian's name.

Me: See if you can get out of her why she's sore.

Lucian: I'll try.

I put my phone away. It doesn't take long before I feel my phone vibrate, but can't take it out because the teacher just walks in. For the next hour, I feel like my phone is burning a hole in my pocket. I just want to check my messages. I don't even hear half what the teacher is talking about. Finally, the bell rings. I grab my bookbag and high tail it out of there. The second that I'm in the hallway, I check my phone.

Lucian: She won't answer. She keeps deflecting like she has been the last couple of days. She also said to leave it alone.

I growl. Why does she have to be so stubborn? What could be so bad that she won't tell us? I pull up Max's name. He can talk to her. He's pretty good at getting people to talk even when they don't want to. He'll probably make some kind of joke and get her laughing and then ease his way to the topic. She won't see it coming until it's too late.

Me: Can you try and talk to Callyn? Luke tried but she's being evasive.

Max: I can see, but if she doesn't want to talk, she won't.

By lunch, no one has an answer and it's irritating. When Callyn sees me walking to our table, she can tell by the look on my face that I'm not happy. It's not like I'm hiding it. She narrows her eyes. The corner of my mouth tilts up. It's cute if she thinks that look scares me. I'm as stubborn as they come, I won't give up on this.

"Callyn."

"Graydon."

I sit. "Are you going to tell me why you're sore?"

"No, and you need to drop it."

"I'm not going to until you tell me."

"And I'm not going to tell you anything."

"I'll just keep bugging you until you do."

"You know what, I don't have to sit here and listen to you. You promised you wouldn't push, but that's exactly what you are doing. I told Lucian to tell you to leave it alone. Why can't you?" Callyn grabs her bookbag and stands up.

"Where are you going?"

"Somewhere away from you."

"Sit down."

"Don't tell me what to do. I get enough of that at home."

I look at her, shock written all over my face. "What do you mean by that?"

Her eyes grow wide, she opens and closes her mouth. Next thing I know she runs out of the cafeteria. I look at the others and they are all sitting there speechless. Zeke snaps out of it first.

"I'll go and find her and make sure she is okay," he says before he gets up from the table and chases after her. My eyes meet Lucian's.

"I just fucked up."

Lucian

Well, that was unexpected. She has so much fire when she gets angry. Why doesn't she carry that all the time? I look over at Graydon. He looks like someone just kicked his puppy. He knows he really put his foot in his mouth this time.

"You shouldn't have pushed. You know what Zeke's mom said."

"I know, but she's so frustrating. I want to know what's wrong, so I can help her. It is really that hard to tell us?"

"Look man. She's just not ready. She has to trust us first. Would you trust a group of people you just met? No. It's going to take time, and you are going to have to learn patience when it comes to Callyn. I hope you learned your lesson about pushing her."

"Yeah," he says as he rubs his hands down his face.

"Let's hope Zeke can calm her down. You're going to see her next period anyway, just apologize. I'm sure she'll forgive you."

He nods his head. The rest of lunch was silent. Zeke and Callyn didn't return. I didn't want to text him just in case he got her talking. I doubt it, but I didn't want to interrupt what was going on, assuming he found her. The bell rings, and we all go our separate ways. I hope for our sake, that Callyn forgives Graydon. He really is a bear to deal with when he's in a bad mood.

.   .   .

Zeke

I book out of the cafeteria. I look around the hall and just catch a glimpse of Callyn's red hair going around the corner. I run after her, and that is a first for me. I never chase girls, but Callyn is different. As my mate, she will always be different. I turn the corner and see her a few feet in front of me.

"Callyn, wait." She turns and looks at me and I see the tears in her eyes. She turns back and starts picking up her pace. "Callyn, please." She stops so I can catch up to her.

"What do you want Zeke?"

"I just wanted to check on you. See if you are okay?"

"I'm fine."

I reach out and cup her face in my hands. I use my thumbs to wipe away the tears. "No, sweetheart, you're not." She closes her eyes and more tears leak out.

"Why did he have to keep pushing? I told him not to and he promised he wouldn't. Why doesn't he just listen?"

"Graydon just wants to help. He likes to fix things. Graydon is a softy, just as much as he is a hard ass. It's his way of showing that he cares." She nods her head. I let go of her face and grab her hand. We start to walk the way to our next class. "He's not just like this with you. He's like this with all of us."

"When I asked him to stop, he should have."

"I know. And I bet you any money he feels like shit."

"Good."

I laugh. "Now, we all heard what you said. Do you want to talk about anything?"

"No. Not yet. I'm just not ready."

I squeeze her hand. "That's fine, but when you are ready, just know that all of us are here. Whatever is going on, it might help if you told someone. We will be more than willing to help."

We end up in front of our class, just as the bell rings. We sit in our seats. A few minutes later Graydon appears in the doorway. He scans the room and spots us. I see his shoulder visibly relax. As he makes his way to us, I see Callyn stiffen. I chuckle. Oh, this girl is going to give poor Graydon a run for his money, and I can't wait to see it.

CHAPTER SEVEN

Callyn

I stiffen when Graydon walks into the classroom. He got me so angry that I let something slip. I didn't want to deal with more questions or answering them, so I left. I knew this was going to happen. I didn't want to tell them anything. I'm afraid that if I do that they'll leave, and I just got them. Graydon makes his way over and sits in his seat. He lets out a sigh.

"I'm sorry Callyn. I shouldn't have kept pushing you. I promise to wait until you are ready to let me know from now on." My head whips over to Zeke and he mouths *told you*. Then he gives me this wink, not an ordinary wink, no it had to be a sexy wink. Yes, there is a difference. I look over to Graydon and see the anguish in his eyes. I sigh.

"I forgive you." He nods his head. I stand and open my arms. He gets up and walks over to me. I wrap my arm around his waist, as he does the same around my shoulders. My head rests just below his shoulder. "My grumpy teddy bear," I whisper. He laughs, like one of those deep belly laughs, and I love the sound.

I pull back and look up to meet his eyes. I like the sparkle that's there now and I'm glad I'm the one to put it there.

"I'll be your whatever you want sweetheart," he says with a wink. I blush. Thankfully the teacher picks that moment to enter and it saves me from having to answer. Graydon just flirted with me, and I have no clue what to do about it.

The rest of the school day passes without incident. No one brought up what happened earlier and some of the tension leaves me. The final bell rings for the day. Everyone goes to everyone's locker, mine being last.

"So, I'll see you guys tomorrow."

"We can give you a ride home, so you don't have to walk," Zeke says.

"No, that's okay." I wave and walk away from them, heading out the front doors of the school. I don't check to see if any of them follow me. I just pick up my pace and to make it home. A few moments later my phone buzzes.

Max: You make it home okay?

Me: Yeah :)

Max: :)

Max: Hey, there is a football game Friday night. You should come hang out with us. You can watch Zeke play.

I sigh. **Me**: I don't think I can make it. Maybe next time.

Max: Aww. :(Okay, let me know if things change.

Me: I will.

I put my phone away and make dinner. My father still wasn't home by the time it was done. I make a plate, grab a bottle of water, and my bookbag and lock myself in my room. I don't know why he's late coming home and I don't know if that is a good thing. Right now, I'll take the solitude. Sometimes I wish he was the type of drunk that went to bars every day after work. But then who knows how he would come home every night. I shudder even thinking about it, let alone what he could potentially do to any other person. Him being home and drunk saves everyone else.

It was later at night when I heard him stumbling into the house. I had left a plate covered on the table for him. Honestly, I don't know why I care. He wouldn't think twice about me, but I know the consequences and they just aren't worth it. I hunker down in my blankets, as I hear him curse. Then it gets quiet, he passed out somewhere. I close my eyes. I found him the next morning, on the kitchen floor, with the plate of food I left, spilled all over the floor.

The rest of the week passes in a simpler fashion. I would hang out with the boys at school and they would offer me a ride home, but I would decline. They all make it a point to tell me how much they didn't like it. I'm just not ready yet. I've only known them a week. But they haven't pushed since the one time with Graydon. They are taking our friendship at my pace. And I've never been more thankful. I would go home and one of them, if not all, would text me. I start to love our nightly texts. It helps me in getting to know them better one on one. My father is starting to come home later and later. I wake up in the mornings and find him passed out in various places around the house. I even had to start waking him up, to make sure he gets to work.

It's Friday and all the football players are wearing their jerseys, including Zeke, and I must say he does look good in it. Every time I turn around someone was bumping his fist or smacking him on the back. The cheerleaders were all trying to get his attention, but he just brushes them off. It was at the end of the school day and we're standing in front of my locker.

"Last chance Callyn. Come out with us tonight?" Max practically begs.

"You know I can't." As much as I wanted too. I almost changed my mind, with my father coming home plastered. I still don't want to chance it though. I sling my bookbag over my shoulder and walk up to Zeke. "Good luck tonight." I give him a quick hug. "Bye guys."

Over the last couple of days, I have been trying to be more open. There isn't much to tell and I don't talk about anything serious. The topic of my father and home life is completely off limits. I've been waiting for the other shoe to drop, with the boys, and with my father. I can't wait until I don't have to constantly worry. Once I leave, I won't care about what happens to him. I won't ever have to take care of him again.

I'm sitting on my bed working on my homework when a wave of texts come in.

Max: This would be more fun with you here.

Lucian: Wish you were here.

Graydon: Zeke looks good tonight. We're winning 24-10.

I start smiling when I see a couple of pictures of them together. One they're serious, another goofing off, though Graydon is serious in all of them. There are a couple of Zeke on the field. Man, he looks good in that royal blue and gold uniform. I save all of the pictures. I'm going to have to find a way to take some with them. I need to figure out a way to be able to hang out.

Me: I wish I was there too.

Me: Looks like y'all are having fun.

I pull up my camera and flip it to the front facing. I hesitate for a moment. Just do it. I take a picture of myself smiling, but I don't like it. I decide to do one pouting because that's more accurate. I really do wish I could be there with them. I end up sending them the pouting picture.

Max: Aww, angel. Don't look so sad.

Lucian: You'll be here next time. Keep your calendar open for it.

Graydon: You're breaking my heart.

I smile. Zeke is right, Graydon is a total teddy bear under that gruff exterior. We text a little bit more and we ended up winning the game. I hear my father walking down the hall. I quickly shove my phone under my pillow. I hold my breath and wait until he walks by my room. This past week, it almost feels like he's forgotten about me. I can't say that I'm mad about that. I know all good things come to an end. After he walks by I release the breath I'm holding. I get up and make sure my door is locked. My father has never abused me sexually, but in the back of my mind, it's there, for me it's always a possibility.

I decide to get ready for bed, changing into some pajamas, and grabbing my phone from under my pillow. I plug it into my charger and get into bed. I wait for the guys to text. They always tell me goodnight and I find it sweet.

Lucian: Goodnight.

Max: Night.

Graydon: Night.

Zeke: Goodnight, sweetheart.

I send them all a text back, but I add congratulations on the win to Zeke's. He immediately replies with a thank you and a smiley face. I smile and place my phone on my nightstand, closing my eyes, I think about the boys as I drift off to sleep.

CHAPTER EIGHT

The Boys- Maximus

I hung out with guys over the weekend, but it felt weird without Callyn. She missed an epic prank I pulled on Graydon. Let's just say it involved Graydon's truck and some post-it notes. There is a prank I want to pull on him in the wintertime that also involves his truck and wet cotton balls. I'm hoping to have Callyn's help on that one. Graydon hates people messing with his truck. We all messaged her to see if she could hang out, but she said she was busy. I don't know, it felt off. I can't wait to see her today. The guys meet at my locker and we are all walking over to Callyn's. I grin when I see her standing at her locker.

"Hey." She jumps and spins toward me. "Ha-ha, gotcha."

"Jesus, you scared me," she said as she placed her hand over her heart.

"Clearly. You okay?"

"Yeah, I'm fine. A little warning next time would be nice." Callyn ducks her head and her hair falls in her face. I reach my hand out to push a lock of her hair behind her ear. She flinches away from my touch. I look over to the others, they all saw and none of them look happy. Besides that, and the first day with us, she has never shied away from our touch. We're careful. She even started to give us quick hugs.

I clear my throat. "So, what did you do this weekend?"

"Oh, you know, the usual boring family stuff. The stuff that you can't get out of."

I don't buy that for a second. "What did you do?"

"Well, I stuck post-it notes all over Graydon's truck. I could have used your help. Do you know how long it took me to place all those post-it notes by myself? Forever."

"What did Graydon do to you to get you back?"

"He put me in a headlock and told me if I touched his truck again without his permission, that he would give me the haircut my mother keeps hounding me about. Plus, he made me take all the post-it notes back off by myself as he supervised." I air quote supervised. Callyn burst out laughing, I mean laughing so hard she has tears in her eyes.

"I wish I could have seen that, and I totally would have helped," she whispers.

"I heard that," Graydon states. Callyn turns and gives Graydon this smile, that I'm going to be trouble smile. "Fuck, we're going to have to make sure those two are never alone together. Who knows what might happen."

I lower my voice and place my mouth next to her ear. We're shifters, so we have exceptional hearing, and I need to make sure Graydon doesn't hear me. "Good, because I have another idea, but it has to wait until winter and I'm going to need your help." Callyn's eyes are full of mischief when I lean back to look at her face. She nods her yes and an impish smile graces her lips. "Do you want to hang out with us this weekend? It's Lucian's birthday."

Callyn looks up shocked, then looks over at Lucian.

"Why didn't you tell me your birthday was coming up?"

He shrugs his shoulders. "My grandma is going to bake a cake and make dinner. That's usually all I do. The guys come over. I don't go out or anything. I would like it if you could come over and hangout with us. Maybe we can watch a movie or play video games."

Is he blushing? Oh, he is. I try so hard not to laugh. I'm so ribbing him for this later.

"I would love to, but I would need a way to get out of the house, and I don't see that as being an option," she says.

"What do you mean?" Graydon questions.

Callyn sighs. "Look, there are some things that I'm not ready to tell you yet. But I will say, I would need a really good reason to leave the house."

Graydon frowns, then says, "Fine, we have all week to figure out a reason."

The bell rings and we all scatter to make sure we aren't late for class. I pull out my phone to message the guys, but I don't get the chance. I just have to wait for third period, and I can talk to her.

👑 👑 👑 👑 👑

The second the bell rings to signal the end of class, I high tail it out of there. I reach English class in record time. I take my seat and watch the door, waiting for Callyn. She strolls in a few moments later. The second she sits down, I pounce.

"Okay, so does this excuse need to be for one weekend or more?"

She just stares and blinks.

"Um. Can this wait until lunch?"

"Well, I guess, but..." I get cut off because the teacher walks in.

I sit back and cross my arms over my chest. I'm just frustrated. All I need is a few minutes to get my idea out. It probably should wait until all of us are together. I see Callyn peeking at me from the corner of my eye. I look over, meeting her eyes. You okay, she mouths. Nodding my head yes, I give her a smirk. Then she goes and does the one thing I'd least expect from her, she winks.

I get it. A wink might not seem like much, but it's coming from Callyn. And damn if it isn't the sexiest thing I've seen.

Lucian

Max is practically jumping out of his seat by the time I get to our lunch table. I have to tell the guys that we are meeting with the Elder Council tonight. My grandfather texted me a little bit ago with the news.

"Dude, do you need a downer?"

"No, but I think I have an idea about how to get Callyn out of her house."

"Really?"

"Yeah, I wanted to talk to her about it earlier, but the teacher walked in and honestly, she didn't seem like she wanted to talk about it." He shrugs. "But it might be better with everyone here. You guys can tell me if the idea is bullshit. Even if everyone likes it, Callyn needs to be on board."

"Do you think that will be hard?"

"What do you think will be hard?" Zeke says as he sits down. No sooner after Zeke sits down Callyn and Graydon join us.

"Max has an idea on how to help Callyn." Everyone turns to look at Max. He's just sitting there nodding like a crazy person.

"I do. But first I need to know if this is just for this weekend or will it need to be longer?"

"Longer would be ideal," Callyn states.

"Okay, the plan is simple. You have group projects. For a month, it can be an English project, the next, chemistry. We can switch what class every month."

"Don't you think her parents will catch on. Who would have a group project due every month."

Callyn clears her throat. "About that, it's only my dad and me. But this could work. My father...let's just say my father indulges himself and probably wouldn't even remember."

I look around at the others and raise my eyebrows. They all shrug their shoulders. Indulges himself? In exactly what way? Sex? Drugs? Alcohol? Gambling? I wish I knew what was going on. That's too many variables I don't like.

"Are you sure? We don't need to make matters worse for you," exclaims Zeke.

"We can test it this weekend. See how it goes. Besides, I'm not missing Luke's birthday."

She looks over and gives me this smile. I can't help but smile back.

Graydon

We talk about the plan a little bit more. Everyone seems to be okay with it, but me. I don't like the idea of putting her in danger. She clearly already is, so why risk it. I'm outnumbered. Callyn said she was comfortable with the idea. She would know better than any of us. I guess we'll see. The bell rings signaling the end of lunch.

"Oh, guys before I forget, my grandfather messaged me, we have that meeting tonight," Lucian says before taking off.

"What meeting?" Callyn questions.

"Oh, it's just about some information we were looking for," states Zeke.

Callyn, Zeke, and I are walking down the hall when some girl purposely bumps into Callyn. The girl whispers something to her, and whatever it is, it was surprising to Callyn by the shocked expression on her face. The girl leaves just as fast as she comes.

I lightly touch Callyn's elbow. "What did she say?" She begins to shake her head like she isn't going to tell me. Oh, no. We aren't doing that. She can keep her home life private, for now, but I'm not doing that here. "Tell me, Callie." She looks up at me at the nickname.

She releases a breath. "She called me a slut and told me to pick one already." She shrugs her shoulders. "I was more shocked that she called me a slut. I don't even know her, and I have no idea what she was talking about. Pick what?"

"I don't know, but we need to get going before that tardy bell rings."

"So, Callie, huh?" she teases.

"I won't call you that if you don't like it?"

"I do. I haven't had a nickname in a long time."

"Why?"

She looks down at the floor before answering. "My mother was the only one who called me Callie. She died of cancer seven years ago. It's nice being called that again."

She looks at me and I can see the unshed tears in her eyes. I open my arms.

"Come here, Callie bear." She giggles. "What? If I'm your grumpy teddy bear, you're going to be my Callie bear." She nods and steps into my embrace.

I just want to protect her. She looks so small in my arms. I want to take away all her pain. I look up and see Zeke smiling and shaking his head at me before he gives me a thumbs-up gesture. The tardy bell rings, shit. I release Callyn and grab her hand and drag her behind me, as we all run to class.

Zeke

Before I know it, it's the end of the school day and we are all piled in my car heading to the meeting that we have with the Elder Council. I'm nervous. The Elder Council has been in effect for almost 200 years. If there is an issue in the shifter community, they are the ones to hand down punishments and rulings. I pull up in front of the office space that the Council uses as headquarters. It's unassuming from the outside. It looks like your everyday run of the mill offices. But unless you are a shifter, you wouldn't know the difference.

We all get out and enter the front door. We each take a seat in the waiting area. I catch myself rubbing the back of my neck. I usually do that when I'm nervous. I look at the others, Max is running his hands through his hair, Graydon is bouncing his knee, and Lucian is looking everywhere but at us. Safe to say that we are all nervous. We wait for what seems like forever, but it was probably only ten minutes, before Elder Harris, Lucian's grandfather, summons us. We enter through a door on the right.

It leads us to what I like to call the judgment room. We pass by a couple of rows of pews, before coming to a stop in front of a long table that has five huge chairs behind it. In those chairs sit, Elders Harris, Caine, Sander, Hastings, and Greaves. It was decided many years ago that there would be five members on the Council, so when they voted on anything there would always be a tiebreaker.

"What could be so urgent, that four teenagers would request a meeting with the Council?" Elder Hastings' voice pulls me from my thoughts.

Lucian bows. "Elder Hastings, the reason for the meeting is because the four of us have found our mate. One female is the destined mate to all of us. She is also a human." Thank god for Lucian.

"Are you certain?" questions Elder Caine.

"Yes."

"This is preposterous. Humans cannot mate with shifters. Humans have no business mating with shifters, creating filthy half-breeds," boisters Elder Greaves.

How dare Elder Greaves talk about my mate this way. My hands clench into fists. Callyn didn't have a choice in her parentage. No halfling does, the bigoted idiot. Honestly, maybe the council shouldn't be filled with such aging, balding, stuffy, old men. They all look similar, with their receding hairlines. The only difference is their eye colors, height, and weights. They even wear the same style robes and in the same color.

"That's enough Greaves. There is clearly a meaning to this. Why would a human be mated to not one but four shifters? There has been no such case of any shifter being mated to not just one but four of us, not since the Alpha Queen," Elder Harris interjects.

"You can't possibly mean what I think you do." Elder Sanders says as he turns in his chair to look at Elder Harris.

"No, but I believe this warrants further investigation. The girl they are claiming to be the mates to, is new to our town. I say we look at our records and see if perhaps she is a shifter but doesn't know it. The shifter gene in her could be diluted to the point she shows no signs." Elder Harris looks at us. "What is this girl's name?"

"Callyn Silvers," Lucian answers.

"We shall have a look and see if we can trace any lineage. But for now, you don't speak a word of this to her. We need answers first. Once we have something, we will contact you. Don't be surprised if we don't find anything. I may need to see her and ask her questions myself. This could help us out in the long run."

"Yes, Elder Harris."

"Good. Continue how you boys have been with her. Don't let her know anything is going on. Also, Lucian, be sure to invite her over some time. I would like to meet her. Give us time to do some research and maybe we'll have an answer." Lucian nods. "You may go."

We do, without another word.

Graydon waits until we are on the road home before he speaks.

"Are you going to do what they said? Not tell her anything."

"They didn't give us much of a choice," Lucian states.

"It feels wrong," I interject.

"I know. I don't like it either, but I don't see another option right now. Callyn doesn't know anything about this world. Maybe we shouldn't say anything to her until we have all the answers and the facts."

Maybe, but it still doesn't feel right.

👑 👑 👑 👑 👑

The rest of the school week flies by. There hasn't been any word from the Elder Council yet and I'm not sure if that is a good thing. We haven't really talked about anything since the meeting. Until we know more, there really isn't anything we can do. We talked briefly about the possibility of Callie being a shifter, but none of us believe that she is. If she was, this would be easier. Like girls leaving her alone because they would know she was ours.

Callyn's had a couple of incidents with some girls over the week. You can tell she is trying not to let it bother her, but it does. Today is the first time Callyn is coming to hang out. I know she's been nervous. She said the conversation she had with her father didn't go well, but in the end, she convinced him. An argument happened between Callyn and Graydon after that about someone coming and picking her up.

Needless to say, she refused, stating that she was more than capable of walking, just like she does to and from school every day. Well, that sparked another argument. One that they eventually compromised on. Callyn said she would let us start giving her a ride home, only after she saw how this weekend, next week, and next weekend went. Then and only then would she let us start taking her home. Graydon tried to throw in picking her up too, but she said they would already be going out of their way taking her home, she didn't want them to do that going to school as well.

Sometimes those two are like oil and water. But then after everything is said and done they makeup by hugging and calling each other by their nicknames. They are seriously entertaining. Graydon isn't used to someone defying him. Callyn gives him a run for his money. Now, we are all sitting here at Lucian's waiting for Callyn to show up when there is a knock on the door. Speaking of the cute little devil.

Lucian goes and answers the door. A few moments later Callyn walks into the room. She quickly glances around, before settling her eyes on us. She smiles.

"Hey, guys." She places her bookbag on the floor and walks over to the couch I am sitting on.

"Why did you bring that?" I motion to the bookbag.

"Had to make it believable. Why would I go to the library to work on my group project but not bring books?" She puts air quotes around group project, then cocks her head to the side, in a duh gesture.

"Well, I definitely didn't think about that."

She giggles and rolls her eyes. Her giggle has this husky sound to it. It's unlike anything I have heard. I groan low in my throat.

"Who is that I hear giggling in there?" Lucian's grandmother asks before walking into the living room. Callyn stiffens, but Lucian goes over and stands by her side.

"Grammy, this is my friend Callyn, I was telling you about. Callyn, this is my grandmother Victoria."

"Well, aren't you just the cutest thing. Just call me Grammy, everyone else does," she says before stepping over to Callyn and pulling her in for a hug.

I see all of us visibly stiffen, not sure how Callyn will react. Callyn surprises us all and hugs her back. Huh? I glance at the guys and see that we each have a look of disbelief.

"Now, Lucian, why didn't you tell me how pretty she is," Grammy said after she releases Callyn.

Callyn's cheek turns so red. Wait, is she blushing? Oh my god, she is. I'm sitting here grinning like an idiot. Oh, I plan on making sure I see that blush on her face daily.

CHAPTER NINE

Callyn

I was nervous walking over to Lucian's. I had to drum up enough courage a couple of days ago to finally tell my father about the group projects. Honestly, it went better than I thought it would, mostly because he was already half drunk when I mentioned it. Plus, I had to wait for him to be home one night. I never know what days he's coming home after work, or what days he's going to, what I assume is, the bar. I like the nights he's at the bar, it keeps him away from me. The only downside is the state I find him in, in the mornings. I shake my head. No more thinking of my poor excuse of a father. I will not let anything ruin this day.

The guys had told me last week that they all live on the same street. They grew up together and were friends from a young age. Their parents get along pretty well too. Turns out they only live three streets away from me and they don't know that yet.

I walk up the sidewalk that leads to the two-story white home. The house has flower bushes in front of the porch and sits on the most pristine lawn I've ever seen. There are four steps that lead up to the front door. I hesitate a moment before I take a deep breath and knock. A moment later Lucian answers.

Oh. Good. Lord.

He's wearing faded out blue jeans, and a tight fitted maroon Henley t-shirt. His copper hair is slightly messy like he just ran his hands through it. I bite my lip as I continue my perusal. He's barefoot. Lord, even his feet are sexy. Can feet be sexy? If so, his definitely are.

Mine.

Woah. Where did that thought come from? I mean, I have this insane urge to touch him... all of them, and to be around them. The sound of Lucian clearing his throat breaks me from my thoughts. I look up and he is wearing this smirk on his face. Apparently, he must have said something, but I was clearly distracted.

"I'm sorry, did you say something?"

"I said, would you please come in?" He steps to the side, so I can enter.

Lucian's house is nice and cozy. There are steps off to the left, when you first walk in, leading upstairs. There is a small hallway and the kitchen is straight ahead. The living room is to the right. Lucian waves me ahead of him.

It should be illegal for people to look this good in a pair of blue jeans. I stare at the guys for a moment when I enter the living room. I mean I've seen them all in jeans at school, but I guess I never really noticed until now. These boys can fill out a pair of jeans! I start to look around the room before they notice I'm checking them out. There are pictures on the wall, and I want to see if any of them are of a younger Lucian or the boys. Before I can go and look, Zeke asks why I brought my bookbag. So, I told him, it's to make this seem legit.

He looks stunned and it causes me to giggle. Before I know it, an older lady barrels into the living room asking who's giggling, calling me pretty, and hugging the crap out of me. She smells like cookies and it comforts me. Reminding me of when my mom used to make cookies for me and I couldn't help but hug her back.

"Make yourself at home. I've got a couple more things to finish up in the kitchen," she says before she leaves. As she walks back into the kitchen, I catch a glimpse of her arms. Are those tattoos? Huh.

"Take a seat," Lucian says as he gestures to the couch. "We were going to vote on what to do. We can watch some movies or play games.

We have board, card, and video games to choose from. The movie collection is under the T.V. in the stand. So, since this is your first time here with us, you get the first vote."

"Um, I don't think I should pick first."

"Why?"

"Well, I haven't watched movies in awhile. I don't know how to play video games." I shrug. "So, my vote would be wasted on board or card games." The boys stare at me with open mouths.

"You've never played video games?" Zeke questions.

I shake my head no.

"Like ever?" Max questions.

"Nope."

"Well, that's what will do first."

"Um, shouldn't Luke get to pick? It is *his* birthday." I say looking over at him.

"I'm fine playing video games."

"If you're sure, but you have to pick which one we play. I don't know anything about it. Speaking of your birthday," I say and hop up off the couch and go to my bookbag.

I pull a card I bought at the store this week. Since my father never goes shopping for food, I didn't even have to hide it. I walk over to Lucian and hand him the card.

"Happy birthday," I say and give him a quick peck on the cheek. When I pull back, I know we're both blushing.

"Thank you."

"Open it."

He does and bursts out laughing after he reads it. Totally worth it. His laugh is amazing. He has one of those laughs that when you hear it, you look to see who it belongs to.

"Oh, it's perfect." He pulls me in for a quick hug.

"Now, I want to know what it says," Max whines. I look to Zeke and Graydon and they are both nodding their heads.

The front of the card has a guy dressed like a sparkly unicorn. The inside says: *Happy Birthday! Act like the ginger unicorn you are!* The card gets passed around and we're laughing by the end. It was perfect. Just like the whole day was.

CHAPTER TEN

The Boys- Lucian

The weekend flew by, Callyn spending my birthday with us, was more than I could ask for. Her card is standing up on my desk in my bedroom. I smile thinking about it. Teaching her how to play video games was entertaining. Let's just say, not her forte. She rage-quit so many times. My Grammy doted on her the whole time. Callyn met my grandfather. He seemed to like her, but she was a little standoffish. I can understand; she doesn't know him or know who she can trust. She must be scared. Callyn met one of the Elders, her fate rests in his hands...their hands. The sad thing is, she doesn't even know it. It's hurting all of us, not telling her. It's a secret that I hope she can forgive us for keeping.

Everyone has been on edge since the Elder Council visit. If Elder Greaves has his way, he will keep us from claiming our mate. In the current state of the shifter world, I can't believe he would deny any shifter their right to be with their destined mate. Regardless of what the Elder Council rules, I won't be giving up my mate. I'm more than positive the others feel the same way.

Speaking of the guys, we are currently walking to Callyn's locker. Rounding the corner, we stop short, she is bobbing her head. I look closer and see that she only has in one of her headphones. I instantly want to know what kind of music she likes. We walk over and Max leans against the locker next to hers.

"What are you listening to?" he asks, beating me to it. She jumps.

"Jesus Max. Really? A little warning next time. But, to answer your question it's "Devil's Backbone" by The Civil Wars. Though I generally listen to everything. The next song on this playlist is "Diamonds" by Slim Thug." She shrugs her shoulders, like it's no big deal.

"Can I see," I ask as I hold out my hand.

"Sure." She tugs on her headphones, then hands me the phone.

I start scrolling through her playlist. "This is pretty eclectic." Rob Zombie, P!nk, Rag'n'Bone Man, Colt Ford, Temptations. There are artists from every genre and era.

"I like what I like."

"Do you mind if I make you a playlist of my favorite songs?"

"Go ahead. I like finding new artists and music. It helps keep me sane."

I create a new playlist and label it Lucian. I start adding songs as she finishes up with her locker. The bell rings and we start walking to our classes. Max and Graydon go their separate ways, as Callyn, Zeke, and I walk to chemistry. I pay attention enough to make sure I don't run into anything. When we get there, I take my seat at the end. We switched Callyn to the middle seat after the first day. I'm engrossed in making the playlist, I don't realize that they were including me in their conversation.

"Earth to Lucian," Callyn says with a giggle.

"Sorry, what did I miss."

"I asked Callyn to come to my game on Friday night. She was asking you, if she walked to your house, could she get a ride with you guys," Zeke states.

"Of course. I could just pick you up at your house, so you don't have to walk at all."

"How about, I'll let you know. It depends on the mood my father is in on that day."

"No problem, just throwing it out there."

I finish up the playlist as the teacher is walking in. I hand Callyn back her phone and she quickly shoves it in her back pocket. I can't help but look. She has a nice butt, but that's not what catches my attention. It's the partial bruise I see on her lower back when her shirt raises up from her movements, that does. I frown, looking back to Callyn's face. She turns and the smile that's on her face quickly disappears. I glance back down to her back. It takes a second, but she quickly figures it out because she tugs the back of her shirt down.

"What happened," I whisper.

"Nothing, I just backed up into the table at home," she whispers back.

It's a lie. She couldn't even look at me as she said it. Zeke looks over like he senses something is wrong. I mouth later over Callyn's head. He gives only the slightest of nods to let me know he understands. I let it drop, for now. We both tried to pretend nothing happened the rest of chemistry, but it was awkward. The second I was out of Callyn's sight, I pull up a group message with the guys.

Me: I saw a pretty nasty bruise on Callyn's lower back.

Zeke: Is that what was going on in chemistry? You guys were acting weird.

Max: Are you serious?

Graydon: Did you ask how she got it?

Me: Yeah Zeke. And of course, I did Graydon.

Me: She said it was from hitting her back on a table.

Max: Maybe she did.

Me: No, you didn't see her reaction to when she figured out what I saw. If it was from a table, why try to hide it? She couldn't even look me in the face when she told me.

Zeke: Could you be overacting?

I shake my head, even though they can't see me.

Me: No, her eyes got real big and she yanked her shirt down so fast and hard.

Graydon: You know she isn't going to say shit. Even if she didn't get the bruise the way she said, do you really think she'll admit to anything?

Max: No.

Zeke: So, what do we do? Nothing? The Council already has us doing that.

Graydon: Any word yet from the Council? It's been a week.

Me: I don't like it, but probably. We can't help until she tells us. And no word from the Council. I have a feeling Elder Greaves will stall for as long as possible.

Max: I got to go. She keeps giving me weird looks.

I put my phone in my pocket. Callyn is so infuriating. I know she was lying; I know it.

Maximus

Callyn has been giving me the side eye since I sat down. I can't tell her that me and the guys are talking about her. After a few moments I can't take it anymore, so I end the conversation. It's not like we were getting anywhere. We're at a standstill from both Callyn and the Council. I make light of everything, but even this is getting to me.

"So, can I make you a playlist too?" I practically beg. Hoping to divert her attention.

I was waiting for her to question me about who I was talking to, but it never comes. Instead, she rolls her eyes at me and hands me her phone. I hide it under the desk. Well, it's easy to spot Lucian's playlist, it's just his name. Oh, yeah. I'm going to name my playlist Maximus the Great. I snicker to myself. As our English teacher drones on about some type of poem, I create my playlist. I finish and decide to look at her other playlists. Lucian is right, there are songs from a multitude of music genres.

I sneak her phone back to her when the teacher goes to write on the board. She quickly grabs it and shoves it in her bookbag. I pull out my phone and pull up my music app. I tap her elbow. Make me one, I mouth and add in a pout for good measure. Callyn gives me this look. Then mouths, 'Really? Now?' I nod enthusiastically. She rolls her eyes again, but quickly grabs my phone and just drops it on her lap right as the teacher turns back around.

A few minutes later I see her fiddling with my phone. She continues until the end of class. We're out in the hallway when she hands me back my phone. I want to see the name of the playlist she created, 'Slytherin In', I laugh.

"Harry Potter, huh."

"It's my favorite. I read all the books. I borrow from the school's library all the time. I haven't been able to see some of the movies though."

"I have them. You'll just have to come over and watch them with me." I waggle my eyebrows.

"I would like that," she says with a smile. It doesn't quite reach her eyes.

"You okay?" I ask as we start to walk toward her next class.

"I will be."

Callyn gives me a small smile before walking into her class. I think about the shadows that haunt her pretty eyes, as I walk to my own class.

Graydon

Callyn was a little reserved during math. She's normally reserved, but more so today than usual. I ask if she's okay, and she says she's fine. I call bullshit. I was hoping that maybe we can all make her feel better at lunch, but I was wrong. She's just playing with her food. I glance at each of the guys, they don't like this either. Max is the first to break the silence.

"So, I had Callyn make me a playlist, after I made her one. Guess, what did she named it?

"What?" I ask.

"Slytherin In," he says and promptly busts out laughing.

My eyes roam over to Callyn and I can see the smirk on her face and the slight shake of her head.

"Is that your Hogwarts house?" questions Lucian.

"Yeah. I went to their official page and took the sorting quiz. Quite frankly, it surprised me. I thought I would have gotten Ravenclaw."

"Wait, a second. Are we just going to ignore that both Max and Lucian made her a playlist? I want to make you one too. Graydon, you should make her one also. Callyn, will you make a playlist for me on my phone?"

"Sure." They swap phones. "Does anyone else know their Hogwarts houses?"

"I do." Max states. "I'm a Hufflepuff." He says proudly.

"You know Slytherin and Hufflepuff are supposed to make good friends."

He nods. "One of my favorite things about being a Hufflepuff is that their dorm room is near the kitchen, easy access to the snacks. We should make the rest take the quiz, so they can find out."

"I know mine." This time it's Lucian. "I'm a Ravenclaw."

Callyn looks up, hands Zeke his phone back. I pass mine to her and Zeke passes me her phone.

"Makes sense. If I had to guess, Zeke I would say is a Gryffindor. Graydon would probably be a fellow Slytherin, though underneath might be the heart of a Gryffindor."

"I'll take the quiz when we have time," I say.

"Me too," claims Zeke.

"There's always study hall. You can pull the website up on your phone," states Lucian.

"See, that's the Ravenclaw in you," giggles Callyn.

By the end of lunch, we each made a playlist on her phone and she made one on ours. The shadows left her eyes and she seems more like herself.

Zeke

I can hear Graydon grumbling under his breath about taking the quiz. I'll take whatever quiz Callyn wants, just so I don't have to see her the way she was earlier. She reverted to the way she was when we first became her friends and I don't like that. I like the Callyn we get to see now, the one that's happy, smiling, and laughing. I love the sound of her laugh. Her whole face lights up and she looks so beautiful.

Focus Zeke. I finish and sure enough, I'm a Gryffindor. I turn my phone to Callyn.

"How did you know?"

"You just show the traits. Brave, daring, courageous."

"What are the traits of your house?"

"Cunning, ambitious, determined."

"Is that why you think Graydon will be in Slytherin?"

"Yeah, the stubborn fool."

We look to Graydon and he has a scowl on his face.

"Why the face Graydon?" I ask.

"Because I got Slytherin. That's the house where everyone is bad or evil."

Callyn scoffs. "Not all Slytherins are bad, just look at me."

He cocks his head to the side and roams his eyes over her body. "I guess you're right."

"Plus, we're in the same house." She moves her fist out for him to bump it. He does and smirks at her.

Callyn breaks through his gruff exterior. He's softer around her, well, is *getting* softer around her. He still likes to push her buttons, but she gives it right back. I think he gets off on it. This girl is 'Slytherin in' alright, right into our hearts. Well, mine for sure but if the look on the guy's faces says anything, she's slithering her way into theirs too.

CHAPTER ELEVEN

Callyn

At least the rest of the week at school was mostly uneventful. I had a couple of girls be jerks, which I have come to realize is because the guys are my friends. I have not seen any of them talk to other girls, or mention going on any dates; and if you believe the rumors now being spreading about me, I'm screwing all of them. For the most part, I ignore them, but it's progressively getting worse. I want to tell the guys, but I don't. Besides, this is a cakewalk compared to what happens at home.

A couple of weekends ago, my father punched me in my arm, because I was trying to help him after he came home drunk as a skunk. I was shoved to the floor and kicked in the ribs after one of the times I tried to wake him up, after I realized he would be late for work. There is a particularly nasty bruise on my back, from when he pushed me into the door handle, because I didn't get out of the bathroom fast enough.

I've been lucky though; I haven't had him hit me with the belt for a while. Lucian saw a bruise on my back earlier in the week. I lied about what happened and I was afraid he would say something to the others. As far as I know, he hasn't and it wasn't mentioned, for that I am grateful. I know I will have to tell the guys what is going on eventually, but I don't want to right now. I don't want the pity they would give me.

Knowing them, they would try to help me, but there is nothing they can do. I don't have anywhere else to go. My mom has a sister, but I haven't seen or heard from her since my mom passed. That's probably my father's doing because they never got along.

I didn't have a phone then, and we have moved a couple of times since then as well. Enough of that, it just depresses me more than my already sad life does. Also, I'm slightly freaking out because I gave the guys my address. Lucian, Max, and Graydon are going to be on their way over, to pick me up, so we can go to Zeke's football game. I am excited to go and cheer on Zeke. It will be my first football game and the boys couldn't be more excited to take me. Lucian messages me that they are on their way. I agreed to let them pick me up, despite my better judgment. So, I grab a hoodie, because it's starting to get chilly at night and wait for the boys outside. One, I can't let them in the house. Two, it will be faster to get away from the house, if I'm ready and waiting. Three, I have no clue when my father might come home. I'm hoping that he's still gone when I get back. If not, I'll have to sneak in, and I'm nervous about that.

In all actuality, I shouldn't be doing this, but I can't seem to help myself. I find comfort and safety when I'm around them. Almost like I know they would do anything to protect me. Insane, I know, but I have felt like we are connected deeper than we know. I don't know, I could just be thinking all of this because I have friends for what seems like the first time in my life. In what seems like no time at all, Lucian pulls up to the front of my house. I hop down the stairs and rush to the car. Graydon gets out of the passenger side and gestures for me to get in.

"I can sit in the back, I don't mind."

"Yeah, I don't mind either," Max says as he pokes his head up to the front.

"No, Callyn gets the front seat."

I slide into the front seat not wanting to argue. The longer we stay out here, the faster we could be discovered. Graydon shuts my door and then gets in the back. Once everyone is buckled, Lucian starts to head to the school.

"I figured I should warn you, I have no clue about anything related to football. So, be prepared for lots of questions."

The guys chuckle. "We pretty much were expecting that," Lucian says.

"It's not too hard to follow. If you come to more games, the faster you will pick it up," states Graydon.

"If you say so."

♛ ♛ ♛ ♛ ♛

I was not expecting this, there are so many people! There are adults and kids with face paint and a whole themed cheer section, which Max tells me is the student spirit section. I can totally see him in the stands as one of the kids with his shirt off and a letter painted on his chest. All the seniors have a banner hanging up. I tug on Graydon's sleeve.

"I want to find Zeke's," I say as I move to the banners. "I don't want to lose you guys. Will you go with me?

"Sure." He grabs my hand and threads our fingers together.

It's an intimate gesture. I'm surprised that not only did he do that, but also because I don't want to let him go.

"Hey, guys Callie bear wants to find Zeke's banner."

The boys nod and Lucian starts to cut through the crowd. Graydon and me follow while Max brings up the rear. We're about halfway down the stadium when we spot Zeke's banner. It's a giant photo of him in his football jersey, senior written across the top, and his last name across the bottom. With my free hand, I take my phone out of the front pocket of my hoodie.

"I want to take a picture of it."

Graydon lets my hand go and I'm oddly sad about it. I quickly take the picture, hoping that maybe he will grab my hand again. Well, if I'm being honest, I kind of want to hold all of their hands. Ugh. I just don't want to leave anyone out. I'm about to put my phone away when Max grabs it.

"Go stand in front of the banner." I do. "Smile." Max takes the picture.

I'm about to go back over to them, but Max stops me.

"Wait, I want to do a funny one and then one with all of us together. Look up at his picture Callie and fan yourself like you're hot."

I do as he asks, and he takes the picture. He starts to chuckle, then faces my phone to Lucian and Graydon. They start to laugh, now I want to see. I go over and wedge myself between Lucian and Graydon. I look at the picture and start to laugh. It's comical and looks so outrageous. Max stops a nearby student and asks if he wouldn't mind taking our picture. We go back in front of Zeke's banner, Lucian on my right, Max on my left, both with an arm around my waist. Graydon is standing behind me with his hands on my shoulders. In this moment, I have never felt so safe and cared for. I know I have the stupidest grin on my face, but I couldn't help it. I never want this moment or feeling to end.

CHAPTER TWELVE

The Boys- *Maximus*

I saw Graydon holding Callie's hand. At first, I thought it was just because he didn't want to lose her in the crowd. When we first walked in there was a cluster of people, but when the crowd thinned out, he didn't let go of her hand. If I'm being honest with myself, I was jealous. Then I remembered that she's not only mine but ours and I have no reason to be jealous.

I take a couple of pictures of Callie, then ask someone to take our picture together. As everyone is getting into their spot, I notice the dude who is going to be taking the picture is checking Callie out. I frown, I don't like that, not one bit. So, after he takes the picture, I grab Callyn's hand and walk over to him. He sees and looks between the two of us. I smile at him, like yeah, she's mine. He hands me the phone and I hand it back to Callie. I look at her and she doesn't seem to mind me holding her hand. She shoves her phone back into her hoodie pocket, before looking behind us to the guys.

"Can we get popcorn? Please," she practically begs.

"Yeah, Callie bear."

"Yes! Thank you!"

We all chuckle. "Come on, let's go get your popcorn, then find some seats," I say.

After paying for a couple of slices of pizza, some pop, and some popcorn, we go and try to find some seats.

"Where do you want to sit Callie," Lucian asks.

"Somewhere in the middle, so I can see everything."

We make our way through the rows and sit near the top of the stadium, at the fifty-yard line. Graydon sits in front of Callie, while me and Lucian sit next to her. We pass out the food and a few minutes later the game starts. We're nearing the end of the first quarter when Callyn starts taking some pictures of Zeke on the field.

"I didn't know he was this good," she exclaims.

"Yeah, he's been playing since he was little. Football is in his blood. There is a good chance he could go pro, but I don't know if he wants to."

As the game continues, each of us has been taking turns answering whatever questions Callyn has and then Zeke takes a particularly hard hit. Callyn sucks in her breath, reaches out and grabs mine and Lucian's hands. She starts to squeeze, damn this girl is stronger than she looks. She is crushing my poor fingers.

"Is he going to be okay? Why isn't he getting up?"

"He'll be okay. He probably just got the wind knocked out of him."

A couple of moments pass, and Zeke gets up and walks over to the sideline.

"See, told you he would be okay."

She lets out a breath. "I won't be satisfied until I can see and ask him myself. Can we stay afterward so I can check on him?"

"Anything you want, baby," says Lucian.

"Good."

I smile to myself. This girl is amazing, and she doesn't even know it.

Lucian

We won the game, and now we are waiting outside the locker room waiting for Zeke. Callie is bouncing around and continuously looking at the door. After what seems like forever, Zeke emerges. Callie runs over and practically jumps on him to give him a hug. He puts his bag down and lifts her. She wraps her legs around his waist and is basically strangling him with her hug.

"Come on, let's go save him."

"I don't think he wants to be saved," chuckles Max.

I take a moment and really look at Zeke. He looks like he's in heaven, with the smile that is on his face. He has one arm around her waist and the other gripping the back of her head. Lucky, bastard.

As we get closer, we hear Zeke say, "I'm fine sweetheart, I promise. I just got the wind knocked out of me."

"I was so scared when you didn't get up right away."

"I can tell, but honest-to-god, I'm okay."

She nods her head, which is in the crook of his neck. Slowly she untangles her legs, and Zeke gently places her back on her feet, not letting go until he knows she is stable. Once he steps back, Callyn finally registers what she did and turns a shade of red I've never seen.

"Oh. My. God. I can't believe I just did that. I'm so sorry Zeke! I didn't realize. I was so worried, that I didn't think about what I was doing. I just reacted."

"Don't sweat it, sweetheart. You can hug me like that anytime you want," and he gives her this wink that makes her turn even redder. I didn't think that was possible. He grabs her hand, "Come on, let's get out of here. I want some food and to sleep."

Zeke holds her hand until we get to my car. He opens the passenger door, she slides in, and Zeke leans down giving her a quick peck on the cheek. He closes the door for her and gives her a wave, then heads to his car. The ride back to Callyn's was quiet. Callyn gets tenser the closer to her house we get.

"You okay Callie?"

"Hm? Yeah, I'm fine."

"Are you sure? If you're worried about what happened with Zeke, don't be."

"Oh, um, no, that's not it. Well, not entirely. I'm just not ready to go home. I had such a wonderful time with you guys. You know, minus seeing Zeke get hurt; I just don't want this night to end." She looks out of her window.

I look up and catch Max's eyes in my rearview mirror. I don't have to look at Graydon to know, we are all probably thinking it. She doesn't want to face whatever is at home. I wish I didn't have to take her back.

Graydon

Lucian pulls up in front of Callyn's and I visibly see her shoulders drop. There is a car in the driveway that wasn't there when we came to get her.

"Whose car?"

"My father's."

She just stares at it for a moment longer, before looking over at us.

"Thank you for taking me with you tonight. I had a blast."

She opens the car door and slides out. After closing the door, she takes a deep breath, almost like she is preparing for whatever is waiting for her on the other side. We watch her walk up to the front door and slowly open the door to peek around. A few seconds later she enters the house. We sit there a couple of more minutes before Lucian leaves. We are all quiet until he pulls into his driveway.

"Did you see that? The way she geared herself up, just to walk into her house." I groan. I'm frustrated with her. She doesn't seem to realize that occasionally, she will let something slip.

"Not to mention she peeked inside before she completely entered. Who does that?" Lucian questioned.

"Someone who is clearly not safe. I think we should subtly start asking her questions. Throw them out there when her guard is down, she has done that a few times," suggested Max.

"It could work. We should get Zeke's input as well," states Lucian.

"I'll message Zeke and see if he's still awake," I say.

Me: Hey man you up?

Zeke: Yeah what's up?

Me: Can you meet us outside? It's about Callie.

Zeke: On my way out.

"Let's go down to his house. He said he'll be outside." Zeke was already waiting by the time we walked the few feet to his house.

"What's wrong with Callie? Did something happen?"

We all shake our heads no. Then we explain what happened and the plan we started to discuss about getting her to open up and finally tell us what is going on.

"I don't know guys. It might work, but if it doesn't and we push her too far," he shakes his head. "Will you all be okay if she leaves? If she stops being our friend? I know I wouldn't be okay. She is slowly opening up to us and she's just now starting to trust us. Are you willing to throw the little progress we have made away?" He has a good point. "She's my mate and I can't watch her walk away from me. Whatever this is, it's bigger than us. This is about her, not us. This is not what we want, but what she wants and needs. We need to be the constant good and support in her life, because she clearly doesn't get that at home."

I hate when Zeke is right.

"So, we wait. I'm with Zeke, I can't lose her!" I exclaim.

Lucian and Max nod their heads in agreement.

I'm not good with waiting, but for my Callie bear, I will try.

Zeke

Shit, I can't believe I just said that but I'm not wrong. Tension is running high because it's obvious to anyone with eyes that something is going on with her. Add in the fact that the Council still hasn't said anything, we're all going crazy. We're not the sit-around-and-wait type, but that is exactly what we are doing. The only reason why I suggest continuing that, is because of Callyn.

When she ran into my arms and wrapped her legs around me, I almost dropped to my knees, nothing felt so good and so right. She hugged me so tight, like she was afraid I would disappear. It hit me like a ton of bricks. My feelings for her are not just because of the mate bond I feel, it's because of who she is as a person.

The only thing I could do was reassure her that I was fine. I hated that she was worried about me, but I can't promise that I won't get hurt again. She was waiting around to check on me, and I realized just how much she cares. I don't think anyone has ever cared when I got hurt. But this girl, who I know is going through some type of hell at home, does; and she has such a big heart.

If I'm not mistaken, Graydon is feeling the same way as me. Lucian and Max didn't say much, just that they agreed to wait. I want to ask the others if they feel the way they do just because of the mate bond, or if it's because of Callyn. The mate bond is strong and the animal half of us uses that bond. But we are still human, and our human selves have separate feelings from our animals. Tonight, is not the night to divulge our feelings.

I sigh, "Guys, I'm beat. Let's give it a couple more weeks, and if no more progress has been made, then we will come up with a plan. I'm tired."

They all grumble but soon head to their own houses. I wasn't kidding when I said I was tired. Chances are soon as I hit my bed, I'm going down for the count. Before I go to bed, I just want to text Callyn. I text her almost every night. It's a need in me, I have too, and now I sound like a crazy stalker. I groan and go to my room and grab my phone that I tossed down when Graydon texted me. I sit on my bed and push myself back until my back is resting against the headboard and my feet are stretched out in front of me. I go to my messages and click on Callyn's name.

Me: Just checking to see if you are okay?

Callyn: How did you know I was just thinking about you?

Thank god she can't see the stupid smile on my face.

Callyn: Shouldn't I be asking you that question?

Me: Ha-ha, I promise sweetheart, I'm fine. I know you're not used to seeing me get hurt.

Callyn: Ugh. I would like to not see that happen again, but I understand that it's not possible.

Me: You still coming over tomorrow?

Callyn: Yup.

Me: :) other than that, did you have fun tonight?

Callyn: I had so much fun. I didn't think I would like football, but I do. I enjoyed watching you play. You're good.

Hell yeah. I love that she likes watching me. I'll play even better, just for her.

Callyn: I took pictures. Want to see?

Me: Of course, sweetheart.

A few minutes later I had at least ten pictures, most were of me on the field. My cheeks are starting to hurt from the constant smiling. I come across the pictures they took in front of my banner. I'm looking at the group one and my eyes immediately go to Callyn. I've never seen her look so beautiful. Her face is flushed from the cold, bright sparkling eyes, and that smile...that smile I would do anything for.

The next picture is just her smiling, standing in front of the banner. She looks just as good. I swipe to the last and it's her pretending to swoon from my banner. I bust out laughing. Once I get myself under control, I save all the pictures to my phone. Then I go to my photos and click on the one of Callyn by herself and set it as my wallpaper, then I text her back.

Me: Those are some great photos. I love the pretend swoon one.

Callyn: Oh, good. I almost didn't send it but thought what the hell.

Me: I'm glad you did. Tomorrow we are going to take a picture together.

Callyn: :) okay

Me: Okay sweetheart, I hate to cut this short but I'm tired. Night, baby.

Callyn: Get some sleep. I'll see you tomorrow. Night.

I get up and pull down the covers. I climb back in bed and plug my phone in. I turn it on, just so I can see her picture. Damn, if she doesn't look good on my phone.

CHAPTER THIRTEEN

Callyn

The next couple of weeks fly by and I got to spend more time with the guys. The more I get to know them, the more I like. They are all creeping their way into my heart. I finally got to meet all their parents and they seem nice and loving. But seeing as how my father is all I have now, I almost forget what it was like having a loving parent. Then I remember my mom and she gave me all the love I needed.

I got good at avoiding my father too, over the last couple of weeks. I only had a couple of incidents with him, and they were tame compared to his usual. I go through the routine I have when I get home from school. I make dinner, grab my stuff and hide in my bedroom, which is where I'm currently at.

I plug my headphones into my phone. I open my music app and select the playlist Lucian made for me. I haven't really listened to the playlists they made me a few weeks ago. because they keep me busy. We hang out on the weekends; they pick me up in the mornings and drop me off after school. I haven't needed to listen to music on the walk to and from school.

I grab my books and start to work Calculus homework. I'm in the middle of solving a problem when a catchy song starts to play. I start tapping my pencil on my notebook and bobbing my head. This song really makes me want to dance. I grab my phone and jump up from my bed. I replay the song and start dancing. I'm not particularly good at dancing, but I don't care, and no one can see me. I start to sway and move my hips. I shake my shoulders to the beat, then my butt. The song plays through, so I put the song on repeat because I want to keep dancing. I feel so carefree at this moment. I smile and giggle. Oh, if the guys could see me. The song replays a couple of times and I'm starting to catch onto the words and start to sing along.

I spin around, and my heart stops. My father is standing in my doorway. His face is furious. Oh god. I should have known better. What was I thinking? I should have never used my headphones because then I would have heard him come up the stairs. I tug on my headphones, and they fall from my ears. He looks at the phone in my hand.

"Where the hell did you get that phone? I sure as hell didn't get that for you. There's no way in hell I would even let you have one," he yells. "Dancing like a whore on top of it. Who taught you to do that? Are you dancing with boys that way?"

He crosses the room in two strides and yanks the phone from my hand, turns and throws it at the wall.

"Answer me," he screams. His breath is heavy with the stench of alcohol.

"I-I-I," I stammer. My throat is thick with apprehension. I can't even get the words out.

He grabs me by the arms. The grip is so tight, that I know I'll have his handprints marking me. He shakes me.

"Why can't you just listen. Is that too hard for you?" He shoves me, my hip hitting the edge of my nightstand. My father walks over to where my phone landed, turning back to look at me quickly before he precedes to stomp on the phone. "I'll make sure you can never use this again."

Please for once let this be the end. I close my eyes and silently pray, but it's not. I hear the buckle of his belt. I open my eyes to see the belt being pulled through the belt loops of his pants. My father folds the belt in half, making his way to me. I brace, waiting for the first strike. The first hits my left side and the second hits my right. I cross my arms around my middle and hunch over. The third hits my back. It hurts so much that I scream, that earns me a fourth. I collapse to my knees, curling myself into a ball. I'm expecting another hit, but it doesn't come. I glance up and my father is looking down at me. His chest heaving, his eyes so full of hate.

"Why do you have to look like her?" he questions, before promptly turning and walking out of my room, slamming the door shut behind him. I huddle into myself as much as I can and cry.

I cry for so long my throat hurts and my muscles are stiff from being in the same position for so long. I force myself to get up. Every muscle is protesting as I do, I hurt everywhere. I glance at my phone and gingerly make my way over and bend down. The moment I pick the phone up, the whole thing falls apart. I start to cry all over again.

👑 👑 👑 👑 👑

I crack open my bedroom door and listen for any movement. It's quiet, eerily so. I open my door just enough that I can squeeze through. I'm careful of the floorboards that creak, as I make my way downstairs. I peek into the living room, checking to see if my father is passed out on the couch. I don't know how many times that has happened over the years. Luckily, he's not there, I sigh. I glance back up the stairs hoping that he is passed out in his bed and not in the bathroom. That has happened countless times over the years as well. I tiptoe to the landline phone in the living room and pause before picking it up.

Is it too late to call? I glimpse at the clock on the wall, it's almost midnight. They are all probably in bed. I shouldn't do this. I should just wait until tomorrow to tell the boys at school. But what if one of them have been trying to get a hold of me? Who would I even call? I start to bite my nails; the indecision is killing me. Just do it Callyn. Pick up the phone and call the first number that pops into your head. I hesitate. Why am I so worried? If they don't answer I can leave a message. I'm going to call their cell phone anyways, that shouldn't wake anyone else up.

Quit stalling. I pick the phone up before I can talk myself out of it. I dial Graydon's number. Probably not my best option, seeing as how he's so surly all the time, but he makes me feel safe. I cross my fingers and hope that he answers. On the third ring, he picks up.

"Hello," his voice raspy from sleep.

"Graydon, it's Callyn," I whisper. There is a moment of silence before he says anything.

"Callyn, are you okay? What number are you calling from? Where are you?"

"I'm fine and I'm at home. This is my house phone."

"Why are you calling me from your house phone? Why are you calling so late? What happened to your cell phone? Are you okay?"

"Um..." I hesitate to answer. Should I tell him the truth? I quickly decide against it. "I accidentally broke my phone. So, if you or one of the other guys tried to text me, that's why I haven't answered. I don't know when I'll be able to replace it. Can you let the others know?"

"Yeah, but how are we supposed to reach you until then? Can we call this number?"

"NO," I practically shout. I wince, looking toward the stairs. I hold my breath for a moment, waiting to see if my father hears. I don't hear anything. I clear my throat, "Sorry. I didn't mean to say it that way. You can't call this number. If I need something, I'll call one of you. My father...my father wouldn't understand or approve. It'll be better for everyone if you don't call here."

"Is that why you are whispering? So, he doesn't hear you?"

"Yes." I look back to the stairs, picturing what would happen if he caught me on the phone this late, let alone with a boy.

"Callyn, what's going on? Don't tell me nothing because your reaction and answers aren't normal."

I sigh into the phone. "There is something going on, but right now isn't the time to talk about it. It's late and we have school tomorrow. Plus, if I get caught," I trail off leaving the rest unsaid.

"Fine. I'll let it go for tonight, but this conservation is far from over. I expect answers tomorrow."

"I know."

"Good. I'll text the others and let them know what's going on."

"Thank you, Graydon."

"Anything for you, Callie bear. Go to bed and try to get some sleep. I'll see you tomorrow."

I nod even though he can't see me. "Goodnight."

"Night, Baby."

I hang up the phone and tiptoe my way back to my bedroom. I quietly close my door and crawl into bed, pulling the covers up to my neck, huddling on my side. I close my eyes knowing that I'm not getting out explaining what is happening. I start to cry. I hope they don't think less of me when they find out that my father abuses me. I cry myself to sleep dreading the morning to come.

CHAPTER FOURTEEN

The Boys- Zeke

Graydon texted us all late last night. He gave a rundown of what happened and that we were finally going to get some answers from her today. I believe him, there is no way any of us could let this slide. I don't like the idea of her being in that house with no way for her to reach us in case of an emergency. We all piled into Graydon's truck today. We were all dressed and ready to go faster than normal. I know the guys are as eager as me to finally get answers.

Now, we're sitting in front of her neighbor's house waiting for her to come out. After what Graydon said we thought it would be better to sit here. We don't want to give her father more ammunition. What seems like hours later, even though it was just minutes, Callyn comes out of her house. She glances up and looks around before spotting us. She walks stiffly all the way to the car. I hop out of the front and wait for her to take the seat I was just in. She slowly gets in and sits ramrod straight in her seat. I close the door. I hurry and get in the back right behind her. I watch as she moves slowly to put her seat belt on.

Don't think I missed the wince on her face from the movement. Graydon must have seen her struggle because he reaches across her to grab the seatbelt. When he does Callyn visibly tenses and tries to shrink in on herself and lets out a whimper. Graydon immediately sits back.

"Callie bear," he whispers.

Ever so slowly she looks up at him. "I'm sorry. I'm so sorry. I didn't mean..." she trails off and starts to sob uncontrollably. "I...I know... I know you wouldn't...I'm sorry," she says between hiccupping sobs.

"Callie bear, I'm going to touch your face." She nods. Graydon gently cups her face, using his thumbs to wipe away her tears. "Take a deep breath for me." She does. "Good. I'm going to put your seatbelt on and we're going to get out of here."

"I can't miss school. They call home."

"Shit, she's right Graydon," I say.

"Fine, we'll go to school, but start talking."

"Where do you want me to start," she says looking out of the window to avoid looking at us. She looks so defeated and I hate it.

"Start with what happened last night," I say quietly.

The more she explains what happened, the more pissed I'm getting. My throat is starting to hurt from forcing the growls down that want to erupt. I want Graydon to turn the truck around and head back to her house, so I can beat the shit out of her worthless piece of shit father. My hands are balled into fists. I want to punch something, preferably her father. With my jaw tight, I look to the others, each of them has the same look on their face. Anger. Hatred. Loathing.

How could her father lay one hand on her? His own daughter, I would never. I can tell you; I'll try my best to protect her. I'll be damned what the Council says, Callyn is my mate. The second I can, I'm taking her away from that hell hole.

Maximus

I have never felt rage like this before. We all knew something was going on, but I don't think any of us thought it was this bad. Callyn was still talking when we pulled into the school parking lot. We wait to get out of the truck for her to finish this story. She goes silent.

"Angel, is that all that happened?" I ask.

"Last night, yes. Graydon's number was the first I could remember. So, I asked if he would relay the message to the rest of you." She reaches to take her seatbelt off, but Graydon stops her.

"I'll get it," he says.

I jump out of the back and rush over to her door. I open it and help her out. The rest of the guys get out. We start to walk, at Callie's pace, into the school. Not wanting someone to overhear the private conversation, I start to ask her about her phone instead. Someone breaking their phone is normal. They just wouldn't know how Callie broke hers.

"What are you going to do about your phone? Are you going to get a new one?" I question.

"I don't know. I don't know when I can get a new one."

"Do you have insurance on the phone, they might be able to replace it for you?" Lucian asks.

"I don't know. I would have to go to the store and have them look it up. I got that phone right after I got my license." She looks around, satisfied no one is listening she continues. "At first my dad didn't want me to get them, but he realized how beneficial it was when we ran out of food. I could go grocery shopping. From there it turned into me making sure the bills were paid because they were constantly getting shut off. He would drink the money away. So, I came up with a way to keep the bills paid. I made a deal that I would make sure the bills got paid and groceries were bought and whatever was left over would go to him, so he could drink."

"Are you fucking kidding me," I say. She shakes her head.

"I also mentioned children services being called and he readily agreed. His drinking got progressively worse over the years. It turned from just on the weekends, to weekdays too. At this point, we're lucky he functions enough to keep his job." She shrugs her shoulders like it's no big deal, wincing in the process.

The bell rings and no one even went to their lockers.

"We got five minutes before the tardy bell," Lucian says. "Hurry. We'll finish this later."

We all scatter, but Callyn. She just turns with her head down and starts to walk in the direction of her first class. My girl is so broken. I rush to my locker and barely make it to my class before the tardy bell. I want to fix this, but I don't know how. I know there is more to come, and I don't know if I can take it. What she's already shared has me twisted up inside. I pull my phone out of my pocket and hit the home button, her smiling face is looking up at me.

It's a candid picture of her and she has no idea I took it. My thumb runs over her face before the screen goes black. I put my phone away. I have feelings for her. At first, I was confused by them. I wasn't sure if I liked her because she is my destined mate or if it was her as a person. The past two months we have grown closer and I realize how much I want to be near her, hear her voice, see her smile, listen to her talk. I love that she helps me prank the guys too. Graydon was right, we are handful when we are left alone together. I can't stop thinking about her. It's fucking Hell not being able to tell her who she is, regarding us. We still don't know much about her and there has been no word from the Council since our last meeting. It looks like we may have to show up randomly. It doesn't look like the Council is going to be too forthcoming with information.

I don't have the slightest idea what to do to help her. Right now, I want to hug her and never let her go. Not doing anything is going against all my instincts as a shifter. My wolf is riding me hard to protect our mate. I have to figure out a way.

Lucian

Callyn was already in her seat by the time Zeke and I got to class. I glance over at her. By looking at her you wouldn't know anything was wrong. But now, we knew, we all fucking knew and did nothing. Why? Because she wouldn't tell us. Plus, the Council has forbidden us from doing anything. We need to have another conversation with the Council. There is no way that they would stop us from helping Callyn now. Shifters value their mates. If the Council knows that our mate is being abused, surely, they will let us act. She told us, that has to be proof enough. I'll take her before the Council so they can see the bruises themselves.

Now, I'm thinking Graydon was right and we should have pushed. I have no clue what we could have done to help. I feel so useless. I want to see how bad the damage is, but I'm afraid to ask. I don't know if I could handle seeing it either.

Taking a closer look at her, I can see how uncomfortable she is. She has pulled her shirt sleeves over her hands and is twisting them. I reach over slowly and take one of her hands in mine giving it a squeeze. She moves her hand and laces our fingers together and squeezes me back. I pull her hand to my lap and hold it until we have to set up our lab equipment. Both me and Zeke have been trying to be gentle and make Callie aware of all our movements. Seeing her break down earlier was enough to last me a lifetime.

The urge to pull her into my lap and shield her was insane. I've never wanted to do that with any girl. I'm looking at her now, and I think it's the first time I'm really seeing her. The beautiful, smart, sweet, kind, loving, broken girl. She's strong, she may not think that right now, but she is. I love everything about her. Callie's hair falls in front of her face and she pushes it back behind her ear. My hand twitches because I want to be the one to do it. Callie looks up at me, probably sensing I'm staring at her like some sort of creeper. She gives me this side smile smirk.

It hits me like a ton of bricks. I like her. I mean *like* her, like her. I want to grab her face and kiss the shit out of her. Oh, fuck. What the hell am I going to do? I can't act on these feelings, not now. I know the mate bond was the initial reason I started to like Callie. But as the weeks go by, and the more I get to know her, the more human feelings start to develop. I didn't know how much until now.

My expression must have changed because Callie is frowning. I smile at her, hoping I'm portraying everything is fine, when it clearly isn't. It must have passed because she gives me a small smile and returns to work on the questions.

Zeke looks over Callyn's shoulder. He meets my eyes, giving me a 'what's up?' look. I just shake my head. It looks like us guys are going to be having a talk as well. Before I know it, chemistry is over. Callie moves to get her bookbag, but I swoop in and grab it before she can.

"I'll carry it. Come on, I'll walk you to your next class. I didn't think about it earlier."

"You don't have to, I'm used to it," she shrugs her shoulders, then makes a face. That move probably just hurt.

I sigh, "That may be, but you have us now, and we're going to help you anyway we can. If that means carrying around your books to give your back a break, then that's what we'll do." We reach her class and Callie looks at me. I can see the tears welling in her eyes. I put her bookbag down. "Please don't cry, baby. I can't take anymore tears. It guts me."

I cup her face and wipe a few of the tears that roll down her cheeks. She sighs and rubs her face on my palm, closing her eyes for a moment as she does.

"Go on. I'll see you at lunch." I bend down and place a quick kiss on her cheek.

There is no way I was going to make it through the day without doing that. I start to walk away but before I turn the corner I glance back, and Callie is just standing there with a shocked expression on her face. Good. Maybe that will take her mind off recent events. She has had too much bad in her life and I want to be the good.

Graydon

Oh, yeah. I saw that kiss. Yeah, it wasn't her lips, but still. That makes three of us, whose feelings now lie beyond that of the mate bond. The animal side of us has separate feelings from our human side and both of my sides are on the same page. We want Callyn. I would bet any money the rest of the guys feel the same. Zeke was smitten after his game, that night. I saw it on his face. I just saw that same look on Lucian's. I'm also pissed because I didn't think to carry her bag for her. What kind of ass makes her put that weight on her back, literally right after she told us her father hit her with a belt across it? Me. That's what kind of ass.

Callyn is staring off into space in the hallway. I get up and walk over to her. I bend down and pick up her bookbag. "Come on, Callie bear."

Her cheeks turn rosy. She must have liked it or is that from embarrassment? How would she feel if she knew I wanted to do the same, but on her lips instead? I frown as I put her bag on the floor and take my seat. What if she only likes one of us? How is she going to feel when we finally do tell her that she is the mate to all four of us? Hell, the others are better suited for her. She hates my rude and pushy behavior, but that's just who I am. Will she give all of us a chance, or will she run screaming?

"Hey, you okay?" she asks, breaking through my self-loathing.

"Yeah, why?" I lie. No, I'm not okay. There is a possibility I have no chance in hell with the one girl I want more than my next breath.

"You're quieter than normal. Well, normal for you anyway," she smirks.

Half of my mouth lifts into a smile. "Yeah, Callie bear, I'm okay. How are you doing? Does your back hurt? Do you need to take anything for pain? Shit, I've been a horrible mate," I whisper, so no one can hear.

"Mate?"

Shit, I said mate. Fuck, play this off, Graydon. "Yeah, mate, you know it's just another name for a friend."

"Okay, mate." She giggles. "And no, you haven't been. Like I told Lucian earlier, I'm used to it. It only hurts when I make sudden movements."

I barely keep a growl from escaping between my lips, when she calls me mate. Hell yeah, I am. I'm just going to have to work hard on making sure I'm deserving of that title. "Do you know how angry it makes me that you're so used to it, that you don't need medicine to help you?"

"There's no sense in getting mad about it. It's not like you could have stopped it from happening."

I groan. "I still don't have to like it."

"Oh, my grumpy bear. I know, but this is going to get worse before it gets better. I haven't even told you guys the half of it. You're really going to blow a gasket later."

Well, shit. I'm not ready for this. Earlier almost broke me. When she huddled into herself in my car, because she thought I was going to hurt her, I almost threw up. The thought of ever laying a hand on her like that makes me sick to my stomach. I wanted to march right into her house and beat her father, the sick bastard.

I'll admit, I love when she calls me her grumpy bear. It does something to my heart every time. It's also kind of funny since I'm a bear shifter. I'll be damned if I admit that out loud to anyone, but her. I have to try to be better, for her.

For her, I would do anything.

CHAPTER FIFTEEN

Callyn

To say I feel horrible is an understatement. No, I don't mean my back. I wasn't lying when I said I was used to it. Before the guys, I would have to walk to and from school with the weight of my bookbag on my back. You get used to the pain quickly, otherwise, it will break you. I can't let it do that. I will escape one day, and I won't look back. I don't care what happens to him after I leave. That might sound harsh, but he doesn't give a crap about me and hasn't since my mother died. Max and I are walking to lunch, another thing I'm not ready for.

To make telling this easier, I'm going to have to start from the beginning. The others are already waiting when we walk in. I take my usual seat, between Max and Lucian.

"Before I continue, let's eat. If I don't, I know I won't be able to when I start." None of them look happy, but they agree.

I eat as slow as I can, trying to prolong the inevitable. The boys...they wolfed down their food. I give them credit for waiting. I sigh, pushing away my food. I can't eat anymore.

"Okay, I told you this morning what happened last night. That is one of many. I'm going to start from the beginning. Whatever I don't finish now, I'll pick up later in study hall. Okay? So, my father didn't use to be like this. He was never overly affectionate towards me, but he was definitely not like this. That changed the day my mother passed seven years ago. The day she died, he basically died with her. When we buried her, I felt like we were burying him right along with her. He couldn't cope with her death. So, he started to drink.

I think to try to forget her. It started off on the weekends. When that didn't work, it turned into every day. I told you earlier about his job. The first time he hit me, was on the one-year anniversary of her passing. He got so plastered that day and from that day forward the beatings got progressively worse. When I was thirteen..." I shake my head. "I'm a girl, and you know, *things* happened." I looked around to see if they understood where I was going with this, they nod.

"So, I had to tell him. He grabbed my arms and shoved me. He yelled at me, that my mother should have been here to deal with my problems. When I started to cry, he punched me in the stomach and told me to suck it up and deal with it. For a while, it was like everything set him off. I started to learn when to try to avoid him. I've been hit for taking too long in the bathroom, for not having dinner done. As I got older, sometimes it would be because I looked too much like her.

The only time he ever hit my face was because I decided to wear makeup. That's where the strict rules came in to play, especially after everyone saw the marks on my face. I wasn't allowed to wear makeup, talk to boys, date, no phones, no friends. No one was supposed to know anything about me. After that, he'd leave bruises in places where people can't see or are easily covered."

I push the sleeve of my shirt up to my elbow, so they could see the bruises there. I quickly pull my sleeve down.

"I've lost count over the years how many times he has hit me, and how many times we've moved because of it. Once someone starts to get suspicious and starts asking questions, we would pack up and move. I've just been trying to make it until I turn eighteen and I graduate. I'm leaving there and not going back. He can't come after me. I'll be an adult."

The bell rings. Thank god. I don't know how much longer I could have talked without crying. The boys are quiet the whole time. I don't know what to make of that. I go to pick up my bookbag but Graydon grabs it and my hand. We start to walk to class. As we walk, neither Zeke nor Graydon has said anything, and I can't take it.

"Say something, anything," I beg.

Graydon comes close. "I'm going to try and hug you without hurting you." He ever so gently wraps his arms around me. "Callie bear, we're just trying to digest what you just told us. We have questions, but those can wait until later. I know me and probably the others are trying to get their anger under control before we do something stupid, like hunt your father down and beat the shit out of him."

"He deserves it."

"I can't argue with you there. But you need us more than we need to go and find him."

He lets go and I'm instantly bereft. We sit down, and Zeke reaches over and grabs my hand and gives it a gentle squeeze.

"We'll always be here for you Callie. If you question anything, never question that," Zeke says softly. He quickly kisses my hand before letting go.

First Lucian, now Zeke. I have no idea what to make of them kissing me. I like it. Boy, do I. I suck in a breath. Oh, man, I think I'm falling for them...all of them. What the hell am I going to do? You messed up Callie. You weren't supposed to fall for them. Let alone all of them. Graydon's gruffness, Max's playfulness, Lucian's nerdiness, and Zeke's calmness. Each so different, yet mine. Oh, man I'm in deep.

CHAPTER SIXTEEN

The Boys-Zeke

We're sitting in study hall, waiting for Callyn. She has gym the period before, and now I'm wondering how the hell she has managed to participate. To say that we are all angry is an understatement. The rage burning in me right now, I shake my head. I've been angry, but nothing like this. It's usually Graydon who is angry, but I think all of us are feeling the effects. This girl has come in and turned this group of friends upside down. I'm wound up so tight. I feel the tension leave me as soon as I see her walk through the classroom doors. How are we going to help her? She can't keep living this way and this has been going on for years.

It takes a strong person not to cave; to get up every day and continue living. How many times has she thought about giving up? How did this beautiful girl survive with no one to talk to, and no one to support her?

No one has said anything since she walked in and sat down. Hell, no one has said anything since we came in and sat down. I don't think any of us know what to do. Suck it up Zeke and be the one to start because it looks like no one else wants too.

I clear my throat. "Sweetheart, is there anything else you need to tell us? Did he do anything else?" The guys shift uncomfortably around me. I hate that I even have to ask, but you never know. If he did, I swear on all things holy, I'll kill that motherfucker. Great, now I am sounding like Graydon.

"No. He has never touched me. Well, not that way."

I let out the breath I didn't know I was holding and the guys semi-relax around me.

"Is there any other family you could call? Why haven't you called the police?"

"I have an aunt, but I lost all contact with her after my mother died. I think my father did that on purpose. I don't remember a time when they got along. I believe he is punishing her by not letting her see me. I'm an only child thankfully, but my aunt is my mom's only sibling. I think about calling the police every day, but I'm terrified of what would happen when he finds out. I don't know where I would go. I'm so close to getting out, that I thought what's a couple more months when I've been dealing with this for years."

Jesus, that's messed up to think. Does she hear herself?

"Baby, you know you don't deserve to be treated this way, don't you?" questions Lucian.

"I know. Before, I was just trying to make it through the day. I was learning how to navigate what my new life was, a life where I no longer had my mother and basically no father. That first year, it was almost like he forgot me. A part of me wishes he did. I would often dream about what my life would be like if my mother was still here. But now...now, I have another reason. You guys, all of you have been rays of sunshine, in my dark existence. You guys are giving me a reason to keep fighting. I don't...I can't lose you." The last part is barely a whisper.

Max is up and out of his seat before she even finishes. She shifts in her seat toward him, turning her whole body. Max kneels in front of her and places his hands on her knees, but she won't meet his eyes. With slow deliberate movements, Max brings his hands up and cups her face.

"Oh Angel, don't you know, I'm not... no, we're not going anywhere. You're stuck with us."

Callyn launches herself at Max. Her arms going around his neck, burying her face in the crook of his neck and shoulder. She lets out a whimper, the move probably pulling on the sore muscle of her back. His arms come around her, holding her close. He looks up and I meet his eyes, he was hurting. I could see the misery in his eyes before he closes them and places his face in the crook of her neck.

I jump at the sound of someone clearing their throat. Our study hall teacher is standing a desk away staring at Max and Callyn hugging. Ms. Neal is in her mid-to-late forties. Her brown hair is graying in the front and is pulled back into a tight bun. Her brown eyes are narrowed, burning holes at Max and Callyn. She has on a shapeless, mid-calf, tan skirt and a blue button-up cardigan sweater. To top off her matronly look, she has on a pair of black, flat shoes. Not the ballet slipper shoes girls wear, but the kind that my grandmother would.

"Care to explain what is going on here?" she says sternly.

Slowly Callyn moves away from Max and sits back in her seat.

"Sorry, Ms. Neal. Callyn got some upsetting news and I was just trying to comfort her. You know to make her feel better," Max says nonchalantly.

"Is that true, Callyn?"

Meeting the teacher's eyes, she says, "Yes."

Ms. Neal must have seen something on Callyn's face because her eyes soften. "I'll let it go this time but try to keep your hands to yourselves." She turns brusquely away and goes and sits behind her desk.

The rest of class we were all model students. The bell finally rings, and I hurry so I can grab Callyn's bag. We make our way out to the hall and I clasp my hand around Callie's. After we stop at everyone's lockers, we make our way out to Graydon's truck. I couldn't go with them because I have practice, but I didn't want to let go of her hand. I was about to help her get in when it hit me, they were about to take her home.

They were throwing her back to the wolf. My entire being went icy.

Maximus

Zeke abruptly stops. Callyn looks at him with a frown.

"You okay?" she asks.

"No. They have to take you home. You have to go back there, back to him. I don't like it. I don't want you to have to go back," he states.

"I'll be fine. Honestly, it would be worse if I don't go home."

Well, damn. I didn't even think about the fact that we would have to drive her home and watch her walk into a place filled with horrible memories. To watch her walk up those steps and enter that house, a house where a monster lives. I feel my wolf pacing in the back of my mind. He doesn't like the idea of putting our mate back in danger. On this, we agree.

"Let's not forget she currently has no cell phone either," Graydon reminds us.

We all growl. This just keeps getting worse. "There has to be something we can do," I say.

"Guys, the only thing you can do now is take me home. Okay? I need to get home in case my father comes home on time. We said I would have to check and see if I have a warranty on my phone, but I can't do that until the weekend. If you want me to do that, I need to go home."

All of us groan. "She has a point," Lucian says.

"Fine," Zeke says sternly. "Come on, sweetheart. Let's get you in the car." He helps Callie in the truck and closes her door. He looks at us, "Make sure she is okay before you leave," he states and stalks off.

Like he should expect anything different. The thought of her being in that house, now that I know for sure what she's going through, has my stomach in knots. Let alone we can't call or text her. Graydon has shared her house number with us, but he said we under no circumstances are to call that number. Now it makes sense why. She has to sneak to use the house phone. I don't want to know what would happen if her father caught her.

I sigh. We get in the truck and buckle up. The closer we get to Callyn's house, the more I don't want to let her go. Before I know it, we are parking out in front of her house. There is no car in the drive. Her father must not be home yet. At least we got her here on time. She unbuckles herself but when she goes to open the door, I reach over the seat and place my hand on her shoulder.

"I don't know if I can watch you walk into that house. How can we just let you go?" I say.

"Because you have too." With that Callyn gets out.

As I watch her walk away, I watch a little piece of my heart walk with her.

.   .   .

Lucian

"It looks like we are going to pay a visit to the Elder Council today, without Zeke. We can fill him in on anything we learn. Once we tell the Council what's going on here, they have to let us do something. They can't just let our mate suffer like this. They can't ask us to sit back and not do anything," I exclaim.

"We need answers. Now," states Graydon, "since we're in the car, let's go straight there."

It only takes Graydon fifteen minutes before he is pulling up in front of the office building that is a front to where the Elder Council conducts their business. No one wastes any time before getting out of the truck and making their way inside. I make my way through the waiting room and straight into the room we were in the last time. Elder Harris and Greaves are sitting in their chairs when we enter the room.

"Lucian, what is the meaning of this?" Elder Harris asks.

"We came to talk to you. We have come into some information we need to share, and we would like to see if the Council has found anything about our mate? It's been weeks and we have heard nothing."

"You insolent child! What information could you possess that would warrant you to barge into the Council chambers?" question Elder Greaves.

"We have found out that our mate has been abused by her father, and this is not a one-time thing. It has happened repeatedly over the last seven years. Now, we came here in hopes that the Council would allow us to extract our mate from such conditions. Surely, the Council would not tell us to stand by and do nothing. This is our mate we are talking about."

"Yes, your so-called mate. Which we know virtually nothing about." The disdain in Elder Greaves voice is apparent.

"You mean to tell me that in the weeks that the Council has been looking for information, you have found nothing?" Graydon growls.

"Graydon," I say his name with a hint of a warning.

"No, this is bullshit. How could they have found nothing?"

"We have found practically nothing about her in the shifter scrolls and ledgers. We have contacted nearby shifter towns and had them look and they have found nothing. There is no mention of any Silvers in any lineage. The only other possibility is that if she is a shifter it's from her mother's side and not her fathers. We would need to know her mother's maiden name before we can do any other research."

"I will get you that information. What about the fact that her father is abusing her? What are we to do about that situation?"

"Nothing."

A deep growl sounds to my left. I look over and see that Graydon has shifted his hands into bear paws and claws, and his eyes are taking on the color and the shape of his bear.

"I'm not going to stand here and do nothing. If that was anyone else, you would have let them rescue their mate. Why are you not going to let us do the same?" Graydon's voice is almost unrecognizable.

"Because she's human," spat Elder Greaves. "If she was a shifter, I would let you take her, but she's not and she has no business being the mate to four of our strongest shifters."

"Greaves, you are seriously telling these boys that they cannot protect their mate? Do you have any idea what they and their animals are going through? Protecting one's mate is like second nature. You are telling them to go against their natural instincts. You have already banned them from telling her what they are, and who she is to them. Isn't that enough?" Elder Harris is looking at Elder Greaves like even he can't believe what he is hearing.

"No. If they want any chance to be with her, they will get the information we need to continue our investigation. If I so much as get a whiff of you boys disobeying an order from the Council, I will make it my personal mission that you never get the chance to claim her." Elder Greaves rises from his seat and swiftly leaves the room.

All of us are stunned and are staring at the door that Elder Greaves just left through.

"I'll figure something out Lucian. For now, keep your distance from the Elder Greaves. Once we have her mother's maiden name, I'll personally look myself. If anything changes, I'll come to you." Elder Harris exits through the same door as Elder Greaves.

"What the hell was that?" Graydon questions.

"I don't know, but Elder Greaves is definitely not on our side. I think he is hiding something."

Max snorts to my right. "What gave you your first clue?"

Now comes the question, do I let my grandfather handle this or do I try and search for the answers myself?

👑 👑 👑 👑 👑

We are all taking this harder than we thought. It's been two days since Callyn told us that she is being abused by her father. We can only talk to her at school because she doesn't have a cell phone and it's been hell not being able to text her. I don't know how many times I have pulled my phone out to message her, just to check on her, to make sure he hasn't done anything else to her. It's been eating at me that I can't. Thank God, we only have to get through one more night. We're taking Callie tomorrow to get a phone. We already talked about it, if she doesn't have a warranty, we're going to pool our money and buy her one.

There is no way she is leaving that store without a phone. The guys are stressing out and trying not to show Callyn, but I think she knows. She's just not saying anything. I find myself looking at her more often than not. I keep thinking about when I kissed her cheek. I was so close to her mouth. It's getting harder for me not to pull her in for a kiss. I want to know if her lips are as soft as they look. I want to know how she tastes.

All of us hold her hand, she doesn't shy away from any of us. I know how I feel about her. I think I started to fall for her when she gave me that unicorn birthday card. Well, the human side of me. My fox wanted her from the moment he laid eyes on her, the first day of chemistry class. I still have the birthday card on my desk, but now there are pictures of Callyn and us along with it. She belongs with us, she fits. She gets my book references, and she jokes around with Max. I love watching her argue with Graydon. He loves it too; I see the spark in his eyes when she stands up to him. Callyn can just relax and kick back with Zeke.

She brings out the best in all of us. Luckily, she hasn't seen the looks she's been getting around school, or so I think. The girls are giving her the evil eye. It hasn't helped that each of us keep turning down every girl that comes up to us. They don't know that she is my mate and that I am spoken for now. Elder Greaves made sure of that. Some of this would be easier if we could just tell people, but we're forbidden. I know there are some shifters who don't like humans. They think shifters are the superior being, but to *witness* the bigotry is different.

We have also had to endure other guys coming up to Callyn. She never seems interested in them, but since she doesn't know that she is ours, she can go out with them. Another problem that could be avoided if we were allowed to tell her. Shifters respect the mate bond. We just head, or in Graydon's case, scare, the guys off. I can't say I'm mad that he does. The thought of her being with anyone else lights a fire in me. It doesn't bother me seeing her with my friends. I trust them. I know she is meant for them like she is me.

Until we can tell Callyn, this is our best option.

Wait, the Council said we couldn't tell her that we are shifters and that she is our destined mate. They didn't say that we couldn't progress our relationship in a human way. A big smile spreads across my face. Wait, until I tell the guys.

Graydon

The last bell rings, thank God, it's Friday. We need to make sure of what time Callyn is supposed to meet us at my house tomorrow. Just one more night and I'll be able to text Callie again. I'll feel better knowing I can talk to her, that I'll be able to check on her. It's been driving me crazy, not knowing, so much so that my dad is tired of my attitude. I finally told him what Callyn had told us, but she wasn't given much of a choice because that asshole broke her phone.

Let's just say my father is furious about Callyn's home life. He absolutely loves her. The few times she's been over here on the weekends, she won my dad over. I can't blame my dad; my Callie bear has won me over too. I love the fire in her eyes when we argue. It's part of why I egg her on sometimes. I just can't help it. She gets so fiery, so alive. Damn, if she isn't beautiful when she's mad. Hell, she's beautiful all the time. I've noticed that all of us have a round-about way of expressing how much Callyn means to us. Callie's voice brings me out of my thoughts.

"So, is ten okay to come over?"

"Yeah, that'll work. It's early enough that the store shouldn't be too busy, and we can hang out afterward."

"Is everyone okay with that?" she asks as she looks at the guys.

"Sounds like a plan," Max says.

"Oh, Zeke, good luck tonight." Callie says with a smile.

"Thanks, sweetheart." Zeke moves closer and pulls her in for a hug, but before he pulls away, he places a quick kiss on her cheek. Callie's face blooms red.

"Awe. Callie bear, are you blushing?" I had to embarrass her further. "It was just a kiss," I say before I lean down and kiss her other cheek.

I never knew someone could turn that red. I laugh, while the guys chuckle. Callie playfully hits my stomach.

"Well, if it's just a kiss..." she trails off.

The next thing I know, she tugs on my shirt and is pulling me down to her level before planting a kiss on my cheek, effectively shutting me up. I can feel the heat rise to my cheeks. The guys are laughing their asses off. Callie turns on her heels, facing off with them. Then, she does something I never expected. She kisses each of them on the cheek. Every single one of us is staring at her.

"Just a kiss, huh guys?" she says with a shit-eating grin on her face.

Lucian is looking everywhere but at Callie, Max is running his hands through his hair, Zeke is rubbing the back of his neck, avoiding eye contact with everyone. Me? I'm stunned speechless.

Someone saying 'Disgusting!' breaks through the silence. I look around to see who said it and my eyes lock on Kelsey Taylor, the school's head cheerleader. She acts like the school's queen bee, but queen bitch is more like it. She walks around here with her mightier-than-thou attitude because her parents have money. She treats everyone like shit. She's been working her way through the football team's starting line. At the end of last year, she had her sights set on Zeke, but he turned her down time and time again. She doesn't take rejection well.

"What did you say," I growl.

Kelsey flips her hair over her shoulder, squaring them afterward. "You heard me. I said disgusting. I can't believe you guys pass her around." She eyes Callyn up and down. "Actually, I can. Just look at her, the trailer park trash."

"You better watch the next thing that comes out of your mouth, Kelsey." My voice is laced with venom. "You can say whatever you want about me, but you will not tear into Callie."

Kelsey opens her mouth, but quickly closes it when she sees all of us move to form a protective wall between her and Callyn. With a huff, she turns and marches down the hall. As one, we turn to look at Callyn.

CHAPTER SEVENTEEN

Callyn

"Has this happened before?" I shrug my shoulders. "Callyn," Graydon growls.

"What do you want me to say, Graydon. I hear this stuff all the time. It's mostly in gym class. I get called a slut and a whore. At first, it was a bet on who I would end up with. Then it turned into who would I screw first. Now, it's how often I get passed around."

"Why didn't you say anything?"

"What would it have mattered? It's not like you can stop people from talking about me. People like her will always talk about people like me."

"What would it have mattered? What would it have mattered she says," his voice rising with each word. "Because it does. You don't need to deal with that shit on top of everything else. What do you mean people like you?"

"It's just words."

I was avoiding the last question. I'm more realistic about how I look. Kelsey has your all-American girl next door look, but a horrendous attitude. She has long blonde hair, bright blue eyes, perfect upturned nose, full lips, and long legs. She always looks like she just stepped out of a magazine. Here I am, pin-straight red hair, brown eyes, and short. She's thin and I'm curvy. I'm always covered up, and she shows skin. I mean I wouldn't show as much as she does, but it would be nice to get a second look.

Sometimes I feel like the guys do things to make me feel better, like holding my hand. Their new favorite seems to be who can make me blush the hardest. Hence, the kisses on the cheek. I don't think they're serious, but a girl can dream.

"Words can hurt, just as much as a hand," Graydon says bringing me back to the conversation.

I blanch. "You know what, I'm done talking to you." Looking over to Max, because he drove today, I say, "Just take me home." I grab my bookbag and make my way to his car.

Those words, I shake my head, they mean nothing to me. I've been hearing them for weeks. Those words don't matter to me. I know what I am and what I'm not. If I show those girls that what they are saying doesn't bother me, they will eventually get bored and stop. Now...now Graydon just messed that up. He showed Kelsey that it bothers them. He just gave her new fuel to add to that fire.

Besides what are a few words, compared to what I go through at home. I didn't like the way he sort of threw that in my face. It's easier to ignore the words than it is to dodge a fist. Thinking about it, I guess he really didn't throw it in my face that my father hits me. He was just making a comparison, and I took it the wrong way. I'll apologize. I make it to Max's car before I turn around.

My guys follow. They keep a few paces behind me, but they are there. They look warily at each other. I sigh.

"I'm sorry."

"I'm sorry," we both say at the same time. I giggle. "No, this was me. I took what you said the wrong way. I took it as you throwing it in my face."

Graydon steps in front of me. "Callie bear, I would never make light of your situation. I should have worded what I said differently."

"Can you guys hug and make-up already? I need to get to the locker room."

"Why are you still here then Zeke? We're fine. Go," I say.

He nods and takes off at a jog. I hold my arms open and Graydon moves that last step. I wrap my arms around his waist and lay my head on his chest. He puts his arms around my shoulders and rests his chin on the top of my head.

"Promise me, Callie, that if Kelsey makes things worse that you will let me... let us, know?"

"I promise."

CHAPTER EIGHTEEN

The Boys- Zeke

I was late walking into the locker room, but there was no way I was leaving before I made sure Callie was okay. I'll take whatever punishment coach gives me. As I sit on the bus on our way home, I wish I could text her. Her not having a phone is a real inconvenience. We lost the game, even though I let my frustration out on the opponent. Graydon isn't the only one pissed that Callyn didn't say that the girls at school were being catty.

I understand where they are both coming from though. We all want to protect her, but we can't be there, or with her, all the time. She needs to know that she can talk to us about what is going on in her life. Those girls may not be a big deal to her, but for me, I feel like that is our fault. We barged into her life and made her a target. But Callyn needs to know that those girls don't hold a candle to her.

I run my hands down my face. I think back to when she kissed my cheek. Her lips felt soft and I wanted to turn my head and see if they felt just as soft on my lips. No one can say I don't have any willpower because that took everything I had. This girl has me all twisted up inside. It's getting harder every day and I'm trying to be patient. Callyn is still healing from what her father did to her at the beginning of the week. Who knows if she can emotionally deal with a relationship. On the outside, she seems so stable. Normal. But who knows how she feels inside.

I pull my phone out of my pocket, along with my headphones. I start my music app and pick the playlist Callyn made. Her music taste is all over the map. Some of the songs I wouldn't normally listen to, but for her, I gave them a try, and honestly some aren't that bad. I let the music play in the background and pull my text messages. I sent out a group text to the guys.

Me: Hey, how did Callyn seem when you left her?

Lucian: She was okay, but you know how she gets when we pull up to her house.

Graydon: I made her promise to tell me if the girls harassing her get worse.

Max: Is there any way we can head this off?

Me: I don't know. I feel like this is our fault. We basically made her a target.

Max: What do you suggest we do?

Lucian: I don't think there is anything we can do. She said it's happening in gym class. We can only stop the stuff that's said in our presence, like today.

Graydon: She needs to speak up and start defending herself. She can't let people keep walking all over her.

Me: I agree. She is starting to do that with us; you especially Graydon. You like to push her buttons.

Graydon: Yeah, but I like seeing her get feisty.

Max: You know, you're not quite right in the head.

Graydon: I mean, when she gets mad, she doesn't have time to overthink anything and she does what comes naturally.

Lucian: She's going to revert every day because she has to go home and hide.

Me: I hate that I can't text her.

Max: It's been hell all week. Luckily, we can fix that problem tomorrow. Are we still splitting the cost four ways if she doesn't have insurance?

Graydon: Hell yeah, she isn't leaving without a phone. I'm not going through another week of this. This shit got me stressed out.

Me: Agreed. We just pulled into the school parking lot. I'll text you later.

Lucian: Before you go, I think I came up with a way to semi get-around the Council.

Max: Do tell.

Lucian: We are forbidden from saying anything about us being shifters and what she means to us, but they didn't say we couldn't date her like a regular human.

Graydon: Hell yeah!!

Max: Sweet! Loophole!

Me: Well damn.

I grab my equipment, leaving my headphones in until I get to my car. I didn't want to talk to anyone. I go through the motions when I get home. I'm lying in bed trying to sleep, but I toss and turn, like I have most nights this week. You got to love Lucian and his mind. This could work out in our favor. Now, to figure out a way that we can all date her and Callie being okay with that. After what seems like forever, I finally start to drift off with thoughts of Callyn on my mind.

Lucian

We have been at Graydon's since eight this morning. I was too geared up to stay home. Zeke and Max trickled in a few moments after I did. Looks like I wasn't the only one. I have been checking my phone, for the time, every five minutes, wishing the time would speed up. Partly, so Callie can get her phone but mostly because I can't wait to see her again. Finally, at ten on the dot, there is a knock on the door. All of us get up and walk to the door, but Graydon answers.

Callyn looks adorable in her hoodie and jeans, her bookbag slung over one shoulder. It's approaching the middle of October and it's starting to cool off. Graydon steps back so Callyn can come in. She sees all of us standing in the hallway.

"You pulled out the welcome wagon this morning I see," she says with a chuckle.

Graydon takes her bookbag and starts to walk toward the living room. He places it by the couch.

"I just have to grab my keys and we can head out," Graydon states.

A few minutes later we are piled into Graydon's truck.

"Did you happen to bring your old phone? There is a chance they might be able to fix it." I ask.

"I have it in my pocket, but trust me, there's no fixing this," she replies.

"Can I see?"

She sighs. "I will on one condition."

"Which is..." Graydon trails off.

"That no one is to get mad. What's done is done. There is nothing any of us can do about this now."

"It's that bad?" Max questions.

Callyn pulls a small Ziploc bag from the front pocket of her hoodie and hands the bag back to me. I was expecting the screen to be cracked, or something that would make the phone useless. But this...this is something else. I carefully open the bag and pull the phone out. When I do the phone falls apart. It's even worse than how mangled it looked in the bag.

"What the hell is that?" Max voices.

"Jesus," Zeke exclaims.

"How bad is it?" ask Graydon. I hold the phone up, so he can look in the rearview mirror. "Fuck, that's not even a phone anymore."

"How did he do that much damage again, Callyn?" This coming from Zeke.

Callyn takes a deep breath. "When he caught me dancing, he grabbed the phone and threw it against the wall. After he berated me, he went over to the phone and kept stomping on it. He said he was going to make sure I wouldn't be able to use it. That's when he took his belt to my back."

"Well, he sure as hell did that," growled Graydon.

I put the phone back in the bag, just staring at it. I'm glad he took out some of his anger on this phone, otherwise, Callyn could have been in worse shape. I glance at Callyn; she has her face turned toward the window. I take a deep breath. I want to pull her onto my lap and never let go. Never let another thing harm her. I will figure it out somehow. I will correct everything with the Council as well.

Graydon

That phone, if you could call it that, was almost unrecognizable. The screen beyond repair, the back was barely hanging on by the wires. The circuit board was broken in half, hanging on by a thread. She's going to get a waterproof phone, and we're getting her one of those life proof cases too. If he did that much damage to the phone, what the hell does her back look like? I don't know if I could see, and not kill the son of a bitch. My hands tighten on the wheel. Between this mess and the bull-shit that Elder Greaves is pulling, I don't know how much longer I have, hell all of us have, before we snap. The rest of the ride to the cell phone store is silent.

I pull into the parking lot and Zeke gets out to open Callyn's door, holding out his hand to help her out of the truck. Over the week, she said her back started to hurt less, but we made it a point to help her, so she didn't jar the injury and make it worse. The rest of us get out. Lucian kept a hold of the phone. Well, there's no fixing that.

"Come on, Callie bear, let's go get you a phone."

An hour later, we walk out of the store, Callie with a new phone and we only paid for a couple of good cases. Lucky for us she had insurance and they replaced it. They were able to recover her contact list, but her pictures were lost. It's a good thing she sent those to Zeke and he can message them back. It's not like we wouldn't have taken more pictures with her. I'm proud of her because when they asked what happened to the current phone, she said her father got angry and smashed it. They gave her a look and she just shrugged her shoulders, not wanting to elaborate. While they worked, we made plans to go to the mall afterward.

"I missed having a phone more than I thought I would. I missed texting you guys every day. I felt like I did before you guys barreled into my life."

"You don't regret it, do you? Becoming friends with us?" Lucian inquires.

"Absolutely not. Before you, I wasn't really living, I existed. I was merely surviving. You all gave me something I didn't know I even needed. I thought I was okay on my own. I mean I have been for years. But having you guys in my life has been the best thing to happen to me in a while. You are breathing new life into me. You are giving me hope. You make facing each day easier."

Well, damn. What do you say to that? I couldn't form any words. Instead, I reach over the console and hold her hand. Callyn is amazing and she doesn't even know it. She has helped and changed us, just as much as she says we do her. The rest of the ride to the mall was quiet. I reluctantly let go of her hand, before I do, she gives my hand a light squeeze. I look at her face and she gives me this small smile. I understood it was comfort.

This time it's Max who opens Callie's door and helps her out of the truck. As we walk through the front door, I realize Max doesn't let go of her hand. My gaze flicks back and forth between the two. Callyn doesn't seem to mind. She looks around as we are walking through the food court, nothing exciting. I look back to Callyn and I see her yank on Max's arm because something catches her attention. I chuckle. At this point, she's basically dragging Max behind her.

"Slow down, Callie. We don't have to rush," I hear him say.

"Sorry, I got excited. Do you know how long it's been since I've been to the mall? Since before my mom passed. I usually go to the thrift store to get clothes."

"Well, then lead on. You don't mention your mom much. And what did you see that captivated your attention?"

"Actually, it was something I thought Lucian would like. Sometimes talking about my mom is hard. I miss her like crazy." She holds out her other hand palm up toward Lucian.

He grabs it and laces their fingers together. Max makes a motion to let go of her other hand, but Callyn doesn't want to let go. She starts to head to the store, pulling both behind her. I look over at Zeke, who is standing next to me, and raise my eyebrow at him. He smiles. I thought maybe we would have a hard time when it came to telling her she is mated to all of us. But now, seeing how comfortable she is with holding two different guys' hands, it may be easier than we thought.

Zeke and I follow behind. When we catch up, I can't take my eyes off the wide smile she's giving Lucian. Her eyes are sparkling. I don't think I've seen her look so happy. I want to see that kind of smile every day.

Maximus

Her eyes grew wide when we walked into the mall. She glanced around the food court but kept walking. Then out of nowhere, she was pulling me towards a novelty store. After telling her to slow down, she explained why she was so excited. I couldn't fault her.

Every time Callyn mentions something else she hasn't been able to do, or her father wouldn't let her do, my heart breaks more. I couldn't imagine having to live basically on lockdown. She's missing out on everything a teenager should be doing. Well, I'll... we'll, make sure she gets to experience as much as she can.

I was surprised when she said the thing that caught her attention reminded her of Lucian. Not because I was jealous, but because her first thought was for one of us and not herself. Then, she extended her hand out to Lucian. When he accepted, I went to let her go, but she squeezed my hand and refused to let go, that was a surprise. So, now we are walking over to the store window, both of us holding her hand. We stop outside of the store and she points, the best she can, with my hand in hers to the mannequin.

She looks over to Lucian and he smiles while shaking his head, but it was Callyn that caught my attention. I've never seen a smile that big from her, well maybe once after we put shaving cream in Graydon's hand and made him slap himself. Right now, her eyes are alight with amusement.

"What did she see?" Zeke asks from behind us. Callie turns enough to meet Zeke's eyes.

"The shirt on the mannequin. It says I'm thinking with a buffer signal. You know because he always seems lost in thought."

"I like it," Lucian says. "Do you want to go inside and look around?"

"Maybe in a little bit. I just want to walk around and see what else is here."

"That we can do."

Over the next couple of hours, we walk the whole mall twice. Once just so Callie could see what stores were here and the next time was her going into almost every store. Normally, I would get bored and irritated having to go inside every store, but Callyn made it fun. Not once did she point out something she wanted. She found a lot of stuff that she thought we would like and made it a point to show and tell us. Her favorite store ended up being the novelty store. It's my favorite store here too. She loved the shirts with the funny saying on them. I like the gag gift section. Halfway through our trip, Callyn went and held Zeke and Graydon's hands and continued walking through the mall, not a care in the world.

Which I've never been more thankful for. She seems oblivious to the looks and the whispers she was getting. Some from older people and some from younger people. Did it look weird that she was holding hands with two guys? Yeah. Did she care? No. Do we care? No. It feels natural, as it should be. We are all mated to her. Once the shifter community knows the truth about us being destined mates, they will understand. The human community, on the other hand, will always give us dirty looks. They don't like what they don't understand. None of that will matter if Callyn and the rest of us are happy.

Callyn was practically bouncing all over the place all day. I was too. The guys probably shouldn't have let us into that candy store. No way was I going to ruin this day, by saying anything to her. She deserves a day to relax, and not worry about what is going on around her. I just hope we made this day special. As we walked the mall, we asked her questions about her mother. We figured out that her mother's maiden name is Cambridge. Hopefully, this bit of information can help us find out more about her past.

CHAPTER NINETEEN

Callyn

This weekend was more than I could have hoped for. I got a new phone, went to the mall, watched some movies, and got to spend some time with my guys. I have never been happier. I love getting my good-night text from the guys at night. I missed those. I hate when I have to leave them. I hate having to come home. All my joy gets sucked out when I enter this house. It's like the house is Azkaban and my father is a dementor. Since, that night a week ago, I have effectively been avoiding my father. It's not like he ever apologizes for what he's done, not like that would excuse it either.

I know the longer I go without having to see him the better off I am. My back has been healing. I try not to let the guys see how it still bothers me sometimes though. The first couple of days after, every time I made a face or a noise, they got the look of murder in their eyes. They have been helping me get through the toughest days. It's honestly such a relief that they know. Once I told them, a weight lifted off my shoulders. I don't have to hide it from them anymore, but they would go postal if I told them every time something happens.

They were ready to hunt my father down after what recently happened. Could you imagine what would have happened if they saw the bruises on my back? The few that they have seen, were already healing and they didn't look too bad. They have been trying to keep my mind off things at home and for the most part, it works, that is until reality sets in. Lord knows what would happen if I get caught.

And it seems like my luck has run out on avoiding my father. I am grabbing my hoodie and bookbag getting ready to go outside to wait for the guys to pick me up for school when my father strolls in the kitchen.

"Why the hell are you still here?"

I quickly snatch my hoodie off the back of the kitchen table chair. I am getting ready to pick up my bookbag, when I get shoved.

"Hurry the hell up and get the fuck out of the way."

I straighten, and my father hip-checks me on his way past. Pain radiates up my hip where the corner of the kitchen table catches me. I frantically grab my stuff and head outside. Luckily the guys aren't here yet. I quickly send a group message.

Me: My father is still home. I'll meet you a street over from mine. I don't know if he'll look outside and I don't want to get caught.

Lucian: Hurry, we'll be there waiting.

I quickly put my phone away and book over. Lucian and the boys were waiting in his car when I get there. They had to be on their way over when I texted. I'm glad I caught them. Graydon jumps from the front and I hop in. He hops in the backseat behind me.

"What happened? Did he say anything?" Graydon questions.

I should just tell them I'll have another bruise, but it's something minor. I opt to leave that part out.

"He asked why I was still there and told me to get out of his way. He didn't say it politely. I grabbed my stuff and immediately left. I texted you guys as I walked away from the house. I was being cautious, because I never know with him."

"I would rather you be safe than sorry. We don't want a repeat of what happened. Hell, I wish you didn't have to go back there," states Zeke.

"You and me both."

Lucian reaches over and clasps my hand.

"Are you really okay?" he asks.

"Yeah, just slightly shaken. I wasn't expecting him to be there. I thought he had left for work."

"That amazes me, the fact he still has a job," grumbles Graydon.

"He doesn't have an option. If he wants to keep drinking, then he must have money. No money, no beer. I don't know how many times I've said that to him over the years. Alcohol is his only motivation."

I hear a few grunts. I didn't have time to question anything because we just pulled into the school parking lot. Lucian hops out the second he puts the car in park. I've learned to just wait for one of them. They got offended the one and only time I opened my own car door. Instead of keeping hold of my hand, he lets it go and I frown.

I understand why he did it, I just don't have to like it. It would just fuel the rumors more. The guys don't care what other people say about them. They are worried about how I would take it. It doesn't bother me. I know people wouldn't say anything, if it was just one of the guys. But nope, I hold all their hands and I kiss all their cheeks. I realized that slowly over the weeks, the closer I get to the guys, the more I like them. I'm crushing on all of them. Yup, that's right all of them and I don't have the faintest idea what to do.

It's not like I have any girlfriends that I could talk to and get advice from. At any rate, they probably wouldn't understand that I feel like I have a connection to all of them. A deep-seated connection, that even I can't explain. The urge to always be around them, to touch, protect, and make them happy, is always present in my mind with them around.

I'm just going to keep on doing what I'm doing, until one of the boys tells me differently. Though I kind of get the feeling they all like me. If that's the case, I wouldn't do anything. No way am I getting in between their friendship. I won't be the reason their friendship breaks apart, I won't be that girl.

CHAPTER TWENTY

The Boys- Lucian

Something is off when Callyn walks into study hall. She was fine all day, and you can tell just by the way she is carrying herself. Her eyebrows are bunched into a severe frown, her shoulders are hunched, and she hasn't even made eye contact with us. Usually, she'll scan the room for us the second she walks in, but she seems distracted. On what looks like autopilot, she makes her way over to her seat. I pounce, the second she sits down.

"Callyn, what's wrong?"

She jumps. "Sorry?" she says sheepishly. "I was lost in my own thoughts."

"Anything I can help you with?"

She sighs. "I don't think there is anything you can do. Kelsey is in my gym class. You know that I have that class before this one." She had four sets of eyes on her, she has everyone's attention. "Apparently, she was at the mall and saw us. Let's just say her comments weren't exactly nice. She said something that kind of hit me hard, and I know I shouldn't believe her, but self-doubt is still there."

"What exactly did she say?" Graydon growls.

"It started off as the usual. I'm a whore, a slut, and I need to stop hogging you and pick one. When I was ignoring her, she upped it, saying I was screwing all of you. Then started the questions; How much I liked being passed around? How much did I charge? Again, it wasn't bothering me because I know the truth. I know showing any sign that what she was saying was getting to me would only make matters worse. So, I continued to ignore her."

"Okay, so what did she say that bothered you?" I question.

"She kept at it the whole period. Throwing jabs here and there. Her friends got in on it and she made sure she said some provocative things in front of the guys, which resulted in lewd and suggestive comments from them. Again, I was trying to not let it get to me, but it was getting harder as class wore on. But after class, when we were in the locker room changing, she started to mention you guys. How you pity the friendless loser, because that's how I would be if you weren't friends with me. The only reason you hang out with me is because I'm easy and I'll let anything between my legs.

Soon you'll get tired of me and send me into an outcast status where I belong. That you guys don't really care about me and that you're just playing games with me. You're just stringing me along. And I know that it's not true, that you wouldn't do that, but it made me question this and myself. What do you guys really get out of this friendship? I feel like I don't bring anything to the table. Why do you guys stick around knowing what my home life is like? Why are you trying to help?"

"There's no easy answer to those questions, Callyn. We have done nothing to make you think we're doing anything but trying to be your friends. Kelsey is a bitch. She's trying to hurt you and get under your skin. She wants what you have."

"I don't have anything. What could I possibly have that she wants?"

"Us," I answer simply.

"He's not saying it to be vain. It's the truth. Kelsey has been trying to wrangle one of us in for the past couple of years. She tried going for Zeke at the end of last year. The beginning of last year it was Graydon. Side note, we are pretty awesome if I do say so myself. I mean have you seen us?" Max says holding his arms out to the side. The grin on his face is the only way you know he is joking.

"You're so full of yourself." I grin back at him.

"She's trying to climb the social ladder. Yeah, her parents have money, but she wants the best of everything and that includes boyfriends. As for why we stick around, it's because we want to. You don't have an easy life, but that doesn't mean you're not worth it, because you are," I say.

"Callie bear, we're here with you because we want to be. Point blank," Graydon says in a matter of fact tone.

"We love everything about you. Everything you have been through, is shaping the person you are becoming. I, for one, am glad you came into our lives. My only wish is that it was sooner. Yes, we know what you deal with at home, but you can depend on us. Have we given you any reason to doubt us?" I say.

Callyn shakes her head no.

"Then believe that we won't. You have to trust us. Trust that we are not going to disappear on you," states Zeke.

"I'm trying, but it's hard to trust others when I couldn't for so long."

"We know that baby, that's why we have been trying to prove to you that you can with us," I say.

Graydon

Fucking Kelsey. We should have known she was going to be a problem, especially after last week in the hall. Callyn knew there were whispers. She even heard the rumors because Kelsey was saying them right to her face the whole time, but she was ignoring it. Then Kelsey goes and unknowingly plays on her insecurities. When we first started talking to her, Callyn had said as much to us. I understood then, because she didn't know us. Going by the reputation that everyone else made for us, we're badasses. We're not really. We stick to ourselves, less drama and trouble that way. But for the past two months, she has gotten to see the real us. She should know that we would never just drop her.

Hell, if I had my way, she wouldn't still be living with her father. But as it stands, right now I can't do anything. The Council, I shake my head, the fucking Council has forbidden me from doing anything. Which is bullshit. For now, I have no clue what to do. She should call the police, but I know the fear and uncertainty of what would happen to her keeps her from calling. I'm being selfish, but I don't want her to leave. I can't lose her. I can't lose my mate. I feel like the worst person for thinking it, especially knowing her father hits her.

Everything that has been said, we heard. We have tried to head some of it off, making it known that no one is to mess with her. But the threats only work on guys, it's not like we can threaten the girls here too. That would make us no better than her father. But Kelsey has a lot of power, and she can make Callyn's life miserable. I hate that Callie still has any doubts about us. What more can we do?

I look over at her as we walk through the halls going to our lockers. She's so beautiful. Why can't she see that? Kelsey, hell no other girl, can compare to her. Callyn is defeated right now. Her eyes are trained on the floor like it's the most interesting thing in the world. She needs to stop moping.

"What's it going to take for you to not doubt us anymore?" Smooth Graydon, just piss her off. Actually, that might not be the worst idea. Everyone else doesn't agree because they all groan. Callyn doesn't get mad though. Instead, her head snaps up and she looks me dead in the eyes.

"Just don't give up on me."

I reach out and envelop her in my arms, my cheek resting on the top of her head. Her arms encircle my waist, squeezing me tight.

"That my Callie bear, I can do. I promise to never give up on you," I whisper.

Zeke

I watch Callie reluctantly pull away from Graydon. She shifts uncomfortably from foot to foot. I have a feeling we are not going to like what she is about to say.

She takes a deep breath. "I have been thinking, and I think we need to stop touching each other so much."

"What?" I exclaim.

"No," bellows Graydon.

"Fuck that," states Max.

"Hear me out. Maybe the rumors will die down, and maybe Kelsey will leave me alone. We fuel the fire because, in some way or form, I'm touching one of you or vice versa. If we stop being so touchy-feely, maybe they'll stop and leave us alone."

"You can't be serious," Graydon growls.

"Is that what you truly want?" Lucian questions lightly.

"No, but maybe people will stop talking about us and being rude ignorant jerks."

"Callie, let them talk! They are going to regardless, there is no need for you to change. If I want to hold your hand, I will. If I want to kiss your cheek just to see you blush, I will," Graydon practically growls.

"I'm with Graydon on this," I state.

"Me three," chimes in Max.

"I am as well," exclaims Lucian.

"Good, then it's settled. We aren't going to change just because some people have a problem. We do what we want, end of story. Are you okay with our touching? Does it bother you?" Graydon questions.

"No, it doesn't bother me. I hated the idea and hated saying it even more. I guess I was just trying to spare you guys. All the girls, and now with Kelsey's help, I'm pretty sure some of the guys too, think we are all dating. I don't want this to be a problem if you guys wanted to get girl-friends."

"Even if we did want a girlfriend, what we have as friends isn't going to change because of that. You were here first, and any girlfriends would have to get used to you too. Don't change because of single-minded people," I say.

"Okay," she whispers.

"Good. Now, unfortunately, we need to get you home."

We drop Callyn off a block from her house because she doesn't know if her father went to work. I'm still reeling from our conversation earlier. How could she think we would change who we are just to please someone else? What people are saying is affecting her more than she wants to admit, and she is trying to be brave about it for us. I admire her for that, but she needs to let us know when things are becoming too much. I want her to learn to lean on us. She can't be brave and do every-thing on her own all the time, even if she thinks she can.

. . .

Maximus

Callyn didn't seriously think we would go along with her plan, did she? How much more is this girl going to go through? She gets physically abused at home, now it's verbal abuse at school. Instead of telling us, she decides to keep yet another thing to herself. Let alone, come up with one of the worst ideas I've heard, and I should know because I come up with stupid ideas all the time. Most of those ideas get me into trouble with Graydon, but he is so fun to pick on. I will never understand why people need to care so much about things that do not concern them. How does my, or the guys', relationship with Callyn make any difference to them. How do we affect them? We don't.

I'm usually the happy-go-lucky one. I try not to take things too seriously. But this is really starting to piss me off. Why won't she just ask for help? People are going to say and think whatever they want anyway. The human people will; the shifters won't bat an eyelash once they know who she is to us. I don't see why she cares. If she is happy, and we are happy, what does it matter? My phone beeps.

Zeke: Guys, what are we going to do about Kelsey? You know she's just going to continue berating Callyn when we're not around.

Lucian: I don't know if there is anything we can do.

Graydon: I wish we had another girl that was a friend that could threaten her for us.

Lucian: I think we have done enough.

Me: What is that supposed to mean? I can totally come up with a prank for her if needed.

Lucian: Just that WE are the reason anyone is coming after her, to begin with. We sat with her. We made friends with her. We are the ones that touch her. Or has no one else noticed she hardly initiates any of the contact? Max don't you dare prank her.

Zeke: No, she hugs us all the time.

I frown. Thinking back, I would have to agree with Lucian, very rarely does she instigate any form of contact. It's usually us, opening our arms to her or us making that first move.

Me: Aww Luke, why do you have to take all my fun away? :(Do you know how epic it would be to prank the school's queen bee? I'd be a legend, but I also have to agree with you, Lucian. Think about it guys, it's almost always us telling her to come to us. There have only been a handful of times that it's been her.

Zeke: You don't think we make her uncomfortable?

Graydon: No, because I asked, and she said she was fine.

Me: Can we be sure? It's not like she's forthcoming with any kind of information. The thing she is comfortable talking to us about is her mother. She lights up like a Christmas tree.

That is a day I will never forget. She looked so beautiful. It was so easy to get information from her about her mother. After she had left that day, we called the Council and gave the information to them. You would think finding anything about Callie's lineage would be easier now, but we still haven't heard anything from them. It's grating on all our nerves. A lot of our issues would not exist if we didn't have to hide them from her and everyone else. My phone beeping grabs my attention.

Lucian: If I hadn't noticed she was off earlier, I doubt she would have said anything.

Zeke: Who knows how long this has been going on.

Graydon: Knowing her she would have backed off and we wouldn't have noticed at first. She would have tried to play it off.

Lucian: That's exactly what she would do.

Zeke: But none of this helps with the situation though. It's not like we can follow her everywhere.

Graydon: No, but we can help her speak up. Maybe if she starts defending herself to others, like she does us, then maybe they'll back off. What the hell is taking the Council so long? We gave them the information that they needed.

Lucian: That could help. It's worth a try. I don't know, I'll try to see if I can find out anything from my grandfather.

Zeke: Okay, but how do we get her to do that?

Me: I have no idea.

I want to help her, but she needs to want to help herself first. Until then, we're just blowing smoke.

CHAPTER TWENTY-ONE

Callyn

No matter how much glowering the guys did, people still kept talking. I figured they would get tired by now, but nope. You think it would, with homecoming approaching. It's still a few weeks out, I thought the girls at school would be more concerned about finding a date, their hair and makeup. Finding a dress and shoes. Don't girls take weeks to plan this? I would like to go, but there is no way I could buy a dress and shoes.

I asked the guys if they were going. Jealousy reared its ugly head at the thought of them going with another girl. It shouldn't, I don't have any claim to them, even if it feels like I do. It still hurt, to think that they would be out having fun, while I hid in my room. Luckily, they said they didn't want to go, because they knew I wouldn't be able to. Instead, we are going to make plans to do something together. Is it crazy how happy that makes me? I feel selfish, but they are mine.

Slow your roll, Callyn. They aren't yours, even if you want them to be.

Right now, we are sitting in Zeke's living room watching *Game of Thrones*. When they found out I hadn't seen it and knew nothing about the show, they said I had to watch it. We are a couple of episodes into season one. This show is awesome. Two words, Jon Snow. When I first saw him on the screen, I sighed. Then I blushed, and the guys start teasing me about it. The guy is hot, sue me!

The doorbell sounds and Zeke hops up to answer. A few minutes later he comes back into the living room holding four boxes of pizza. Thank God, because I'm starving. Lucian goes to the kitchen and comes back with some paper plates, napkins, and some bottles of water. Graydon passes around plates, while Zeke opens a couple of boxes and sets them on the coffee table.

I grab a slice of buffalo chicken and pineapple pizza, because pineapple *does* belong on pizza, and a slice of cheese. I settle back into my seat to continue watching the show. Max grabs some slices and sits next to me. I give him a smile and pick up a slice of my pizza. Just as I am getting ready to take a bite, Max grabs my wrist and brings my hand closer to his mouth and takes a bite, the shithead! I giggle.

Graydon comes around and thumps him in the back of the head. "You have your own, don't eat hers," he says before coming around to the other side of the couch.

"Yeah, but hers is better." Max gives me a wink.

Before I know it, I'm stuffed. Somehow, I manage to sit with my back pressed against Graydon and my legs stretched across Max's lap. I can't say I'm mad about it. I look to find Lucian sitting in front of the couch, but his head is resting on the cushion. Zeke sitting next to him. When did they move? I just want to run my fingers through Lucian's hair. I want to know if it feels as soft as it looks. I shift slightly. I lift my hand but bring it back down.

Just do it Callyn, he won't care. So, before I could chicken out, I lift my hand and slide my fingers into his hair. It is just as soft as I imagined. I spread my fingers out and slowly pulled them back in, massaging his scalp as I do so. I feel him push his head back into my hand. I take that as a good sign and continue to do what I was doing.

A few minutes later, I heard him let out a little moan. I feel Graydon and Max stiffen. They look over and see what I am doing then instantly relax. I wonder what that was about. I did that a while longer before my hand gets tired. Lucian looks back to me.

"You can do that anytime you want, that felt good." I blush.

"Aww, now I want to know how it feels," Max whines. "Me next."

"Too late, I'm already on the floor," Zeke says, as he scoots closer and rests his head on the cushion like Lucian.

"Fine, but I'm after Zeke."

"How about you see if she even wants to massage your scalp first, before you make assumptions," Graydon barks.

"You don't mind do you, Callie?" I look at Max and see he's giving me these big puppy dog eyes. I couldn't help but laugh. It was adorable, if slightly ridiculous.

"No, I don't mind." I crane my neck back to look up at Graydon. "I'll even massage yours if you want."

The corner of Graydon's mouth turns up. "We'll see." I give him the biggest smile I can. He is definitely going to let me.

I did end up giving each of them a massage. They, in turn, repaid the effort. Lucian and Max each massage a foot. Zeke massages my head, and Graydon lightly massages my shoulders. It was the best day of my life until my reality came crashing down. I had this amazing life outside of that four-walled prison I call home. Outside of that house, I had the life I only dreamed about. The kind of life I probably would have had, if my mother was still alive. I may not be friends with the guys, but I would be normal, and that is the only thing I truly want.

My father has other ideas. I never understood why he wants to keep me locked away. Why can't I go out and do normal things? It's probably because he thinks that I'm going to run and tell someone, but he has me too afraid to do that. The uncertainty of what would happen to me is another reason. I don't know where my aunt is, or what kind of foster family I could have ended up with. What if I got one just like my father? Then everything I did, would have been for nothing. I know I sort of tell the guys things, but that took me almost two months to tell them anything. Honestly, if my father hadn't destroyed my phone, I doubt I would have said anything to them. I mean maybe eventually, but not that soon.

Just like when I got home tonight. I was on cloud nine from the day I had with my guys. I always peek around the door when I come home from spending time with them, I want to avoid my father. I slowly open the front door listening for any sounds. When I don't hear any, I quickly enter the house and close the door behind me. I rush up the stairs to my room. Normally, if I hide, he doesn't come looking for me. I seem to anger him when he can see me. That's usually when he will push me into something or punch me.

I thought I had escaped him tonight. Out of sight out of mind, but no, I had to go to the bathroom. I went about my business. I opened the door and ran smack into my father. Let's just say my night ended badly, and now, I'm going to have to wear a long sleeve shirt to school. I will, until the bruises on my lower arms fade. Sometimes I think the guys were brought into my life right when I needed someone the most. I always dreamed of being able to leave, that's my plan, but I honestly don't know if I would have gone through with it. But my guys, they give me a reason. They give me hope; and hope is a dangerous thing.

CHAPTER TWENTY-TWO

The Boys- Maximus

Monday mornings always come too soon, but on the bright side, I get to see Callyn. She was evasive yesterday, saying that she couldn't get away. It's happened before, but I still missed her. Instead, I blew up her phone with text messages yesterday. I was to the point where I was sending her random pictures of myself, and funny memes, though I did get back some cute pictures of her. My favorite was her blowing a bubble with gum but doing it cross-eyed.

I immediately saved the picture and made it the background on my phone. Speaking of the cute devil, she's standing at her locker. I take my time walking over so I could admire the view, it's my favorite. She has on her favorite black boots; she wears those things every day. Yeah, that's right I noticed. My gaze travels up, to her maroon colored jeans. Man does she fill those out nicely, if you know what I mean. She has on a light coral, long-sleeved shirt with silver snowflakes all over it. Her long red hair is straight and down. Callie has one of those hourglass shaped bodies.

Seriously, how the hell did no one notice her at all her other schools? Even if she wasn't my mate, I would have still noticed her. I would have talked to her and gotten to know her. She's so beautiful inside and out.

The other guys haven't caught up with me yet, so I get Callie all to myself, for a few minutes anyway. I take advantage of her being distracted. I come up behind her and wrap my arms around her waist. I give her right cheek a quick peck before setting my chin down on her shoulder.

"Morning Angel."

She turns her head to the side and looks at me through the corner of her eyes. She gives me a smile. Her lips are right there, and all I want to do is kiss her.

"You know, I almost was going to elbow you. You're lucky you said something," she says with laughter in her voice.

"Aww, Callie you wouldn't really do that would you?"

"Probably not, because then I would have felt bad."

"Felt bad for what, and why are you still hugging her Max?" Graydon asks.

"I said I was going to elbow him, but he was lucky he said something to me when he wrapped his arms around me."

"He would have deserved it, so don't feel bad. Again, Max enough with the hugging."

Next thing I know Graydon is pulling me away from Callie. I frown, I like her being in my arms. She belongs there, she fits perfectly; she is made for me. I turn to look at Graydon. Is he jealous I was hugging her? I think he is. She is his mate too, so there is no reason for him to be, but she doesn't know that yet. I wonder how she will take that news. I smirk, it's going to be good. Since I can't find that out yet, I'm going to rile up Callie.

"You didn't mind did you, Callie?" I ask.

She shuts her locker and turns to face us. "No, I didn't. I like your hugs, Max." Callie turns to face Graydon fully. She narrows her eyes and puts her hands on her hips. Now, I wait for the show. "Now, Graydon didn't you just tell me not that long ago that we shouldn't change how we are with each other? Did you change your mind? I like his hugs. I like yours too." She looks over at me. "Would you have asked Graydon to stop hugging me, then forcefully remove him from me?"

"No, I would have just whined until you gave me a hug as well," I reply with a shrug of my shoulders. It's true. I'm not going to lie.

Callie looks back to Graydon. "See, all you had to do was ask for a hug and I would have given you one."

Lucian and Zeke walk over.

"What did he do now?" Zeke asks.

They both look over to Graydon who has a sheepish look on his face.

"I'm sorry Callie bear. I just... I just." He trails off, looking down at the floor.

"You just what?"

"I just...I was jealous and wanted a hug." Callie smiles at him.

"Oh, my grumpy teddy bear," she says before she launches herself at Graydon.

He catches her around her waist. Her feet are off the ground and her arms are around his neck. She leans in and gives him a quick kiss on his cheek. His eyes whip up to meet hers and she just smiles at him. She moves her face so that they are cheek to cheek. I see her hug him tighter. She pulls back, and he sets her on her feet. Callie takes a step back.

"We got to work on your morning skills," she says with an impish smile. "Now, apologize for being rude."

Me, Zeke, and Lucian burst out laughing. Callyn is making Graydon apologize. This girl is the best.

Graydon

Is she being serious? I look at her face. Fuck, she is. I narrow my eyes at her. She's just standing there with a smile on her face.

"What if I don't want to apologize? It's not like I hurt him."

"Apologize or no hugs for a week."

My eyes widen before I narrow them. "You wouldn't."

"I would." She narrows her eyes right back at me.

Of course, Larry, Curly, and Moe are laughing it up at my expense. Do I want to go a week without her hugs? No. I sigh.

"I'm only doing this because you asked, and I'm not going a week without any of your hugs." I turn to Max. "I'm sorry," I grumble. That sends them all into another laughing fit.

"I think Graydon is going soft. Is the pretty girl making you have feelings?" Max says in a baby voice. I growl.

"That wasn't so hard, was it?" Callie asks before she gives me another hug. The bell rings, thank god.

I'm sitting in English, thinking about what just happened in the hall-way. Callie surprised me. I didn't expect her to run at me, but that hug she gave me was awesome. I can't believe she kissed me. When she looked at me smiling, I wanted to kiss the shit out of her. I wanted to feel her lips on mine so bad at that moment. It would have been perfect. Instead of just doing it, I did nothing. I wonder what she would have done.

Would she have kissed me back? I want to believe she would have. One of these days I'm going to find out. Those thoughts carry me through my morning.

We're all sitting at our usual lunch table. Max is teasing Callie when she reaches to grab something from him, but he moves it out of her reach. As she is stretching her arms out, her shirt sleeve rides up. She is too distracted by Max to notice, but I did. I saw the purple marks. I reach over the table and gently take a hold of her wrist. Callie stops and puts her focus on me. I push her sleeve up more. Five purple spots encircle her forearm.

I pull the sleeve down. "Give me your other arm." She does. The guys quiet down. I know they are wondering what is going on.

I gently take her wrist in my hand and with my other, push her sleeve up. Another set of five purple spots encircle this arm as well. I hear some colorful words from the guys. I pull her sleeve down before I let go. I watch as she pulls on both sleeves trying to tuck her hands in. She brings her arms close to her body, practically hugging her middle.

"What happened Callie?" Lucian calmly asks.

She won't meet our eyes. "I got up to go to the bathroom. I was just leaving and when I opened the door, my father was there. I bumped into him. When I lifted my arms, he grabbed me. He was squeezing my arms and shaking me, as he was yelling at me for being in his way. Then he shoved me away from him."

"Jesus, is this why you didn't hang out with us on Sunday?" Zeke asks.

"Yeah. I didn't want to chance anything."

I'm sitting here frowning. I'm so pissed. I get more so each time he leaves another mark on her skin. I lift my eyes and meet Callyn's. She gives me this look, asking if I'm mad at her.

"I'm not angry at you Callie bear. All the rage I'm feeling right now is directed solely at your father, the worthless piece of shit."

I see her nod her head. I get up and go to her side of the table. I help her stand and pull her in for a hug. My hand goes to the back of her head, threading my fingers through the hair at the nape of her neck. My other arm is around the top of her shoulders.

"I promise, baby. I'm not mad at you." Then I move my head until I can whisper in her ear. "I will find a way to help you. Once I do, I promise to make sure no one ever lays another hand on you like that again."

I knew as soon as I said them, it was true. I will do everything I possibly can to keep the promise I just made to Callyn.

Zeke

He left his fingerprint marks on her. It pisses me off. I heard what Graydon said, and I couldn't agree more. I want to sink my teeth into her father's throat and rip it out. I'm sick of him touching my mate, hurting her, leaving marks on her. The damn Elder Council won't let us do anything about it. It's been a couple of months and they are still no closer to having any answers. It sets me on edge. Being near her, smelling her scent, touching her, is strengthening the bond. I can feel it, and if I can the others can. I don't know how this is affecting Callyn. She doesn't know what we are.

Forbidden from telling her until the Elders can get to the bottom of the mystery that surrounds Callyn. I force a growl back. It's been hard keeping some of my animal instincts and urges at bay. The hardest being the urge to claim her. I want to mark her, so everyone knows that she's mine...ours. I can feel my canines lengthen. I need to calm down. I don't want to scare her. I take a couple of deep breaths. I start to feel more under control, and my teeth start to shorten.

Graydon walks back around the table to take his seat. Callyn clears her throat, shifting in her seat. I take another deep breath and scent her arousal. I bite my lip from groaning out loud. What the scent of her does to me. Now, it's me shifting uncomfortably in my seat.

"So, homecoming is next week. Are we all still going to hang out on Saturday?"

"Of course. What do you want to do?" I ask.

"I don't care, as long as we are all together."

"We can go to the diner in town. Maybe see a movie?"

"Oh yes, can we? I haven't been to a movie theater in years."

"Anything for you, sweetheart."

The smile she gives me. I can never say enough about it. It makes me and my wolf happy that we made our mate happy. I almost feel like preening. My wolf wants to rub up against her skin, get her scent all over him. I smile back. Callyn's eyes drift over my shoulder, and that smile falls. I see her eyes narrow, but she quickly looks away. I look over my shoulder and see Kelsey. That she-bitch is causing trouble. She should know better. We have tried to drop hints to her, thinking that she is smart enough to figure it out. I guess not. She knows that once a shifter finds their mate, they want no other, they will touch no other.

It's like she is purposely goading Callyn. Callyn isn't a shifter, that we know of, and Kelsey thinks she is human. She knows Callyn doesn't understand our ways. Kelsey is capitalizing on that. I look back to Callyn and she's just playing with her food. I wish I could tell her she has nothing to worry about. If she was a shifter, she would already know. Callyn glances up and I can see her visibly stiffen. I can smell Kelsey approaching.

"Hey Graydon," Kelsey says as she runs her hand across his shoulders.

He tenses. If Callie was a shifter, Kelsey wouldn't even attempt to touch him. Any shifter female would attack another female for touching what is theirs. I can't wait to tell Callyn. She thinks Kelsey is just a pampered princess, the most popular girl in school, like this is a normal high school. It mostly is, and Kelsey is pampered, but mostly because she does come from a high-ranking family. Most males here would beg to get attention from her, and they do, but to her, they are not good enough. There are some shifters who get together because of the power and prestige they gain from the pairing. Some are lucky to find their destined mate, but most aren't.

Before Callyn came into our lives, Kelsey was trying to land one of us. Max's family is the best at agility, Graydon's family is known for their strength, Lucian's family has been on the Council for years and are all highly intelligent, and mine is fighting. We excel at predetermining an opponent's next move. We train shifters; make them better.

For the last two years, Kelsey has been trying to get one of us to pair with her. Once I got...we got a whiff of Callyn, that was it. Stick a fork in us, we're done. Callyn is everything I wished for in a mate and more. She is perfect for us. I can't wait until I can shout it from the rooftops that she is ours. I have to agree with my mom, Callyn was given to the four of us, to make up for the shitty life she has had; for the lack of love. We are going to give her all the love she can handle, fourfold.

Lucian

I don't know how Graydon can stand having Kelsey put her scent on him, let alone her hand. Graydon comes from a long line of strong bear shifters, known for their strength and determination. For him to not shove Kelsey's hand off him and immediately go to Callyn to replace the scent, is amazing. That takes a lot of willpower. I know it's mostly because Callyn doesn't know about us, what we are. It's getting harder every day to keep it from her.

I've been groomed my whole life to one day take the spot on the Elder Council. The spot that my grandfather currently holds. The pursuit of knowledge has always been ingrained in my family. If anyone can find the answers we need, it's the Council. But until they do, we are not to pursue Callyn in any official capacity, which is going against our baser instincts, that of our animals. Graydon shifts enough that Kelsey's hand falls away from him.

"What do you want Kelsey?" he questions. She pulls out the chair next to him and sits down. She pushes her chest out a little and flips her long, blonde hair over her shoulder.

"You know that the homecoming dance is coming up, and I was wondering if you have an idea of who you were asking to the dance."

She puts her hand on his forearm, but Graydon moves his arms and crosses them over his chest, a nice subtle move. I know what you must be thinking, shifters having a homecoming dance, how human of you. While there are a few humans who attend this school, there are more shifters. Our homecoming dance is nothing like the human one. Well, it sort-of is, but there is more to it. We invite neighboring shifter towns, to see if anyone can find their destined mates, or to see about a mutual pairing. The humans have no clue what is really going on.

New shifters come to town all the time, looking for their destined mates. We show up in couples, more for show, but if someone finds their mate or a better potential mate, they go to that person. Honestly, it would be better if we showed up separate, but we keep up appearances because there are a few human families in town.

"I'm not going," Graydon says.

"What? What do you mean you're not going? You have to!" Kelsey says affronted.

"No, I don't," he says with a shrug. Kelsey quickly recovers her composure.

"Well, I thought we could go together," she says and places a hand on his thigh. Graydon is up and out of his seat, the second her hand touches his leg. Graydon is reaching his limit. He walks over to the other side of the table, pulls up a chair, and places it as close to Callyn as he can, then sits down.

"You've gotta be kidding me. She's the reason you're not going. Really?" He just lifts his shoulders.

"We have plans." Kelsey narrows her eyes at Callyn. She moves over a seat, sitting next to Zeke.

"What about you Zeke? Who are you going with?"

"I'm not going either." She turns and looks at me.

"Before you ask, I'm not going," I say to head her off. I hear a snort and a slight chuckle. It was from Callyn. Kelsey hears it too.

"What do you find so funny?"

"Just the fact that you sound desperate and can't take no for an answer." The second that she says it, she slaps a hand over her mouth.

CHAPTER TWENTY-THREE

Callyn

The second those words come out of my mouth; I regret it. What in the world has gotten into me? I should never have said anything, but I couldn't take seeing her paw all over Graydon. Then she set her sights on the others.

They. Are. Mine.

There go those thoughts again. They aren't mine, but I have a hard time seeing her or any other girl touch them. I have this urge to rip out her throat, and I have no idea why.

"Well, you would know all about being desperate wouldn't you, vying for the affections of four guys. You little..." The rest of her words are cut off because one of the guys growls.

When I say growls, I mean *growls*, like a dog.

"If I were you, I would watch the next thing you say about my ma-about her," Graydon says venomously.

He was going to say something else but corrects himself. I look around to everyone quickly and it seems like only the guys knew what he was about to say; I make a mental note to ask later. Kelsey is too busy glaring at me.

"Can't even stick up for yourself, weakling."

She basically spat the last word at me before leaving. I look at the others, I could see their faces contorting with anger. She really got under their skin.

"So..." I was beginning to say but got cut off by the bell. I wait until me, Zeke, and Graydon are walking to art class before I finish asking my question. "So, did any of you date Kelsey?" I don't like the idea one bit.

"None of us has," Zeke answers me. I relax, relieved by the answer. I hate the idea of her hands on my guys. "Why do you ask?"

I shrug my shoulders trying to play it off. "No reason, she just seems hell-bent on hooking up with one of you. I figured she already dated someone, and was trying to make one of you jealous, or get one of you back." I was trying to downplay it, but I hated the idea of one of them touching her, being with her. I don't understand the jealousy I feel.

"There is nothing to worry about. We don't want Kelsey." Zeke puts an arm around my shoulder, then kisses my temple.

I couldn't help but lean into his side. I want to bury my nose in his neck and inhale his scent. He smells like pine and sandalwood, a scent I could roll around in. I want to nuzzle against his chest. I stop myself; barely. I love the feeling of being in his arms, I love being in all their arms. I sigh.

"You okay Callie bear?"

"Yeah, I am."

I go over to Graydon and put my arm around his waist. His arm goes around my shoulders. I love his scent too, freshly mowed grass and earth. I know that sounds weird, but he smells like outside. I want to nuzzle him too.

"You guys smell good." My face is flaming. Oh God, why can't I shut up?

"Oh, yeah? Well, we think you smell good too." Graydon kisses the side of my forehead.

There really is no better place to be.

"Oh look, if it isn't the whore herself."

Kelsey. I guess what happened at lunch bothered her. Just ignore her, Callyn. I am walking by her when she grabs my arm and shoves me up against the gym lockers. Until now, she has never laid a hand on me, all she did was talk trash. But today must have really pissed her off. I went to move around her, but she put her left arm across my chest holding me in place. Her right hand goes to my throat, the tips of her fingernails digging in.

"You need to start backing off those boys. They are too good for you. One of them will be mine, do you understand? You need to leave them alone. You need to convince one of them to go to the homecoming dance with me."

"No." Could you be more stupid Callyn? This chick has you by the throat and you're telling her no. "I won't help you. They clearly don't want you, so stop. Now, you just look pathetic, pining away for someone who doesn't want you." Well, the boys keep saying I need to stand up for myself. What better time, since I keep putting my foot in my mouth today.

Kelsey grips my throat tighter, squeezing, cutting off my oxygen. I bring my hands up to wrap them around her wrist. I try to pull her hand away from my throat, but she is scary strong. I try to use my nails and dig them in her arm, trying to scratch her. Kelsey doesn't even notice.

"Do. Not. Mess. With. Me. You will do as I say, or next time I won't be so nice. Do you understand me?" The edges of my vision going black before she lets go and I slump to the floor. Taking in big gulps of air. "Look, right where you people belong, kneeling at my feet."

Kelsey turns and walks out of the locker room. I stay where I am and start to cry, my throat hurting in the process. After a few minutes, I muster up enough courage to look in the mirror. I see the red marks from her hand and the indents of her nails across my neck. The boys are going to flip when they see this. Shit so will my father.

CHAPTER TWENTY-FOUR

The Boys- Graydon

I can sense the discomfort radiating from Callyn the moment she enters the room. She clears her throat and holds her head high as she walks toward her seat. I can see the marks on her neck before she fully makes her way over. I narrow my eyes, barely restraining the growl in my throat. Someone dared to lay a hand on my mate, left marks on her. This time it wasn't her father. This time I can do something about it. The others stiffen around me and I know that I'm not the only one who has seen the marks. I wait until she sits down, shifting slightly to take in the scents on her skin.

Kelsey.

This time the growl does escape me.

"Callyn, explain," my voice deeper than normal.

She sighs, "Kelsey cornered me in the girls' gym locker room. At first, she grabbed me and pushed me into the locker. When I went to go around her, she pinned me to the locker, wrapping her hand around my throat. She told me to back off you guys, that you're too good for me. That one way or another one of you is going to the dance with her and I was supposed to help make that happen. She said that one of you is going to end up with her."

"That doesn't explain the marks Callie," Zeke states.

"I might have talked back, and told her no, I wouldn't do what she says. I called her pathetic and she started to choke me, digging in her nails. She threatened me. This is the first time she has physically touched me; I'm chalking it up to the fact we, or me, pissed her off at lunch."

"That doesn't make it right for her to accost you," Lucian says.

"I know, but what else am I going to do? I've had enough from her. She knows that I'm weaker than her. That's why she keeps doing what she is." Callyn shrugs her shoulders.

"You're going to back away from us, aren't you?" I growl. Callyn snorts and looks at me.

"Like any of you would let me. Remember last week? The only thing is, I don't know how to deal with Kelsey. I feel like she's only going to escalate. Then what am I going to do? You can't be in the locker room with me. Today she waited for everyone to leave before she confronted me. I know why, it was so there were no witnesses. It would be her word against mine."

Callie has a point. We can't be in the locker room with her, but maybe we can find a girl in her gym class who would be willing to keep an eye out on her, for us. It'll be hard without telling the female why we need her to watch Callie, but Callie was right, Kelsey isn't going to stop. We need to go and see the Elders today, to see if they are any closer to finding out about Callyn. This needs to stop, now.

We need answers, and the sooner the better. The need to protect her, to claim her, is riding me strong. I know if it's affecting me this way, it must be affecting the others the same way. I can't wait to get out of here. I need to shift and clear my mind. We decided after the last time Callie came to school with bruises, we would take turns going to Callie's home and checking in on her. We may not be able to tell her exactly who we are to her, but that doesn't mean we can't be near. She has a nice set of woods behind her house.

We go for an hour or two just listening. When we think she'll be okay for the night we leave. I've seen her staring out of her bedroom, searching. She can feel someone out there, watching, lurking. She's drawn to us, but she doesn't know why. I can feel it. No way this is one-sided. I'm getting impatient.

"You know we want nothing to do with her, right?" Max says, the need to reassure his mate.

"I know, it's just sometimes hard to believe. I'm not special. Kelsey is beautiful and strong. She is everything I'm not."

If the Elders would just let us tell Callie that she's our mate, then she wouldn't need to doubt herself. She would know we don't want any other female. This is bullshit. I'm almost convinced that the Elders know what's going on and they don't want to say anything. I'm done waiting. One way or another I will find the answers.

Lucian

"No, you are everything she wishes she could be."

Could she use a little more self-confidence? Sure. But she can't get that if people keep bringing her down. Until we can figure out this situation, she's going to keep doubting herself. Callyn looks at me, trying to read my expression. I hope she can see in my eyes what I say is true because once she knows she's my mate... our mate, we will make sure not a day goes by that she doesn't know how much we want her.

She sighs. "I want to believe you and maybe one day I'll get there, it's just not going to be today. Now, I have to somehow hide this from my father."

"Shit," Graydon exclaims, "I didn't even think about that."

His eyes meeting each of ours. We can see the concern. All this stops when we claim her. When we announce that she's our mate. The Elders have had almost two and a half months to find answers. I want to know what is taking them so long. Looks like I need to have a talk with my grandfather. The bell rings and we all quietly shuffle our way into the hallway. We hit everyone's lockers and file into Max's car. The ride to Callyn's is quiet. When we pull up, Callyn practically jumps out of the car and races toward her house.

None of us stop her. We know she needs to do what she needs to, so she can hide from her father for the night, but Max doesn't drive off.

"One of us needs to stay. I can't leave her alone right now. Her father is too unpredictable. What if he sees those marks? There's no telling what he would do to her," Max says.

"I'll stay," Zeke says.

"The rest of us need to go and see the Elders," Graydon states.

"I want to talk to my grandfather alone, maybe he can tell me something. Something he wouldn't in front of the others." They look at me.

"Do you think he would?" Max questions.

"I need to tell him about Kelsey, maybe that will persuade him," I say with a shrug. "Either way, we need answers. I don't like being kept in the dark, not with more threats. We need to protect her, and the Elders are keeping us from doing that and I want to know why."

👑 👑 👑 👑 👑

We left Zeke back at Callyn's. He went into the woods behind her house and shifted. Contrary to the books that humans read about shifters, we can shift fully clothed. It's part of the magic that lets us shift to begin with. If anyone comes through the woods Zeke would smell them, and vice-versa if it were a fellow shifter. The rest of us are waiting for the Elder Council. Half an hour later we're escorted in the Council's chambers.

"Lucian, Graydon, Maximus. What brings you here to see the Council today? Where is Zeke?" Elder Caine questions. Graydon steps forward and bows.

"Elder Caine, we left Zeke to guard our mate. The reason we have come today is to see if there have been any developments regarding Callyn Silvers?"

"We have our researchers digging through the archives. That will take time. As of now, we have nothing new to report. Why does your so-called mate need guarding?" I can see Graydon tense. The Elders are not happy with the idea that a human is a destined mate to a shifter. Let alone that she is the mate to four of the best families at that. Max steps forward. He takes over before Graydon can lose his temper.

"Elder Caine, besides the continued threat of her father at home, she is now getting threats at school. We left Zeke to guard her long enough to know that no harm will come to her this night."

"Very well. Once we find something, we will summon you here. Until then, try not to get too attached to the human." Elder Caine stands and exits through the door behind the council's desk. Elders Greaves, Sanders, and Hastings make a quick exit. Elder Greaves has the same look of disdain on his face as Elder Caine. Elders Sanders and Hastings look back quickly with sympathetic looks on their faces.

I step forward and look at my grandfather, the last elder remaining. "Elder Harris."

Maximus

"Come now Lucian, no need for such formalities. There are no other Elders in the room."

"Yes, Grandfather."

"Now, I want to know who at school is targeting your mate."

"Kelsey Taylor. We have told Kelsey repeatedly that we are not interested, but she will not take no for an answer. She has taken to speaking degrading things to my... our mate when we are not around. Today Kelsey physically accosted Callyn by leaving marks on her throat."

"I see."

"No, grandfather, I don't think you do. I feel like if we were to say that Callyn is our mate, Kelsey would back down. I feel this will only escalate if left alone for too long."

"That may be the case, but who's to say things wouldn't be worse if Kelsey knew? What if she tried to challenge Callyn? We do not fully understand what Callyn being here is supposed to mean. We are trying to keep this quiet for as long as possible. We want to find the answers, to make sure we are fully prepared for any eventuality."

"Yes, Grandfather. Is there anything you can tell us?"

Lucian's grandfather lowers his voice. "What I tell you, cannot leave this room. Well, tell Zeke but make sure no one else is round." We all nod. "We have found a mention of her mother's maiden surname. Just one. We are trying to find the right scrolls to trace her lineage. There is a possibility she may be a descendant of a shifter family. Her blood may be too diluted to have any shifter qualities. Until we find those scrolls, we have no way of knowing.

There is one other thing. We found a book of prophecies; one the

Council did not know about. In that book, it was foretold that a single female would be born and would mate with the four strongest families. By combining the families, this will make a true alpha pairing. This alpha pairing would then bring about change. Some people will not be happy about this change. It will bring a war upon us. This is a critical time. Be mindful," with that Elder Harris whisk from the room.

I look at Graydon and Lucian, both are shocked by what was just revealed. Graydon shakes his head.

"Not here."

We pile into my car and head to my house. On the way, I texted Zeke and told him to meet us there as soon as possible. Zeke is already waiting by the time we get there.

"Everything okay with Callyn?" I ask.

"Yeah, her father still isn't home. It might be one of the days he stays out late. What is so urgent? I can feel the anxiety coming from all of you."

"Let's go inside first." Everyone shuffles in behind me. I do a quick search of the house and no one else is home. "Well, we went to see the Elders. Elders Caine and Greaves don't care what happens to Callyn like we didn't already know that. Elder Caine told us not to get too attached. He also claimed that there was nothing new to report, but Lucian's grandfather straggled behind. He made a good point about why not telling everyone just yet about Callyn was a good idea. We forgot that once we announce, people can challenge Callyn for her position."

"But we are destined. Everyone hopes to find their one. Do you think that someone would really challenge a destined mate?" Zeke inquires.

"Yes, especially after the second bit of information that was passed along."

Lucian took over and recounted to Zeke about the prophecy. His face visibly pales.

"They think it's Callyn, don't they?"

"My grandfather did not say, but that is the route I would take. She is the only one who fits the bill. The four of us are her mates. Also, Callyn may have shifter blood after all. They found a mention of her mother's maiden name. They don't have all the details pertaining to that, but they suspect she is a descendant of a shifter family. It just may be diluted because of the breeding with humans, but we don't know for sure."

It makes sense. Some of the Elders and some shifters would not be too happy if a change was brought about. Some believe too much in their antiquated ways. But too many shifters are settling with a power pairing, instead of trying to find their destined mates. It has brought shifter numbers down; less are being born every year. There also hasn't been a prophetess in many years. At least none that we know of. I know why that book was hidden. No one wants to know a war will ensue. If that prophecy is right, Callyn and the four of us, will bring about that change and lead us into war.

No pressure.

Zeke

This is not what I expected to hear when I got that text earlier. A true alpha pairing, and I could be a part of it. The last known true pairing was about two centuries ago. When that alpha pairing died, turmoil ensued among shifters. The Elder Councils were formed to keep the peace. An alpha pairing could possibly bring an end to the Council, meaning that the alpha would once again rule over the shifters, making decisions for the betterment of all.

The possibility it could be us, Callyn and the four of us, I shake my head. No one can know about this. This could put Callyn in even more danger than she already is. No one knows what events took place that night. Didn't they know the damage that one single act would cause? Magic is dying, fewer shifters born every year. We are dying out.

How the hell are a bunch of almost eighteen-year-olds supposed to lead a war and win? We need answers. We need to know for sure that it's Callyn. How could it not be, all the signs are there. This explains why the Elders didn't want to say anything. Who wants a war? But things must change. If we have any hope for a future, there needs to be a change.

The only thing that was said that was not a complete shock, was that Callie is our mate. I knew that the moment I scented her. The heady scent of vanilla and strawberries drawing me in like a moth to a flame.

There aren't too many destined pairings, but they said you would know the second you meet your destined mate and they were right.

I knew...we all knew. Now, we all had to prepare ourselves for a war. I run my hands down my face.

"What kind of proof are they looking for to prove Callyn is, or isn't a shifter?" I ask.

"The Elders found a mention of her mother's maiden name. My guess is they are looking through old scrolls, at family trees, trying to trace back her lineage. Until they find something, there is nothing we can do. I doubt Callie would know anything," Lucian states.

"There has to be a way to find out. We need answers now. If she is...if we are, the ones the prophecy is talking about, we need to start preparing."

"No one knows what happened that night, all those years ago. No one has been able to find any written records of the account. Why would someone start a war to change the course of shifter kind? The only plausible explanation is power. We do know that a true alpha pairing holds, and wields, a lot of magic. Each member of the pairing brings the best of all talents; strength, agility, knowledge, etc. It is said that the female holds the magic. She helps enhance each of her mates' abilities and helps distribute the magic to all shifters. It's a delicate balance of give and take.

You tip the scales in one direction too much, and the whole thing will crumble and fall. For the Alpha Queen and her mates to be overtaken, it would have taken time and planning, hitting them at their most vulnerable. To this day no one knows what made them that weak. I believe if we can solve that riddle, the rest of our questions will be answered."

"Magic." They all look at me. "Someone would also have to be strong. They would have had to have a following. You can't just barge in and try to take on an alpha pairing that's a suicide mission. Whoever did this knew when to attack, how to attack. How could someone gather more power? By using magic. But how do you gather more magic?"

Lucian's eyes grow wide. "You siphon it," he whispers.

"Shit," Graydon growls.

"How do you siphon magic?" Max questions.

"The most common way is by a talisman. You spell it, and it could gather small amounts of residual energy from around the wearer. Before the magic started to fade, it was said that it was everywhere. You could feel it in the air, the trees, the earth. It's what helped the healers long ago. They would be able to draw in that energy, to help heal people. The only way to create a talisman is by blood magic."

"Fuuuck," exhales Graydon.

My thoughts exactly. Blood magic is dark and evil. Once you make that choice, there is no coming back. Chances are that the talisman is still out there somewhere, in someone's hands.

CHAPTER TWENTY-FIVE

Callyn

Luckily, my father wasn't home the day that Kelsey came at me. I wore scarves and turtlenecks all week, until the bruises started to fade. Thankfully, the weather has started to turn cold, fall officially making its presence. I'm okay with that, it's my favorite time of year. This weekend is homecoming, and me and the guys made plans to hang out all day Saturday. I can't wait. I stayed home this weekend; man was it boring!

I love being around my boys. I'm drawn to them; have been from the start. I hate being away from them. Whenever I'm around them I feel like I can breathe again, I feel safe. It's a feeling I don't want to ever let go of. The boys have refused to let me back away from them. I've even encouraged them to find dates for the dance, but they are adamant that if I wasn't going, they weren't going. Honestly, I can't say that I'm mad. The thought of them touching, or being with someone else, feels like a knife in my heart.

Kelsey hasn't touched me or confronted me again. I think the boys had something to do with that. They made it clear that day they weren't going, and half of the female population, and maybe some of the male population at school, didn't take that well. Kelsey has been giving me the evil eye every chance she gets, like right now from across the cafeteria. If looks could kill, I'd be dead on sight.

"Earth to Callie."

Max is waving his hand in front of my face. I have no idea what the boys are talking about, and apparently, they have been trying to get my attention. I've been so lost in my thoughts; I didn't know they were talking to me.

"Sorry, what did you ask?"

"Oh, my little space cadet," Max teases. I narrow my eyes at him. He just laughs at me. I sigh.

"We were just asking if there was anything else you wanted to do on Saturday."

"No, I'm okay with our plans. Am I still meeting everyone at your house, Max?"

"We're going to meet at Lucian's instead." I meet Lucian's eyes and smile.

I love his grandmother, she's old-people-goals. His grandfather is quite intimidating. He's some kind of judge or something. He sits on this Council. He's nice and friendly, but he just has this presence about him. It's weird but I feel like there's more to him than meets the eye. I feel that way about the boys too.

"Will your grandmother be there? I just adore her." All the boys chuckle.

"No, she has her book club that morning. But I can tell you, she loves you too."

I smile at him. I like all their parents. Zeke's mom is seriously the best cook hands down. My mouth waters when I think about her bacon wrapped, feta burgers. When I first met Max's parents, I thought they would have been stuck-up because they look like they have money, but that was the furthest thing from the truth. They are seriously chill. Graydon's dad, he's the type of dad I wish I had, supportive and loving.

The bell rings, interrupting my thoughts, startling me. I hear Max laugh.

"Yup, space cadet." I playfully smack his chest. He gives me a quick kiss on the cheek. "I wouldn't have you any other way," he says before he walks away, heading to his class. Lucian shakes his head, with a smile on his face. He gives me a quick hug before he leaves going to his class. Graydon moves to my right and Zeke moves to my left, as we walk down the hall heading to our class.

"So, what has you so spacey today?" Zeke asks. I shrug my shoulders.

"You know, just thinking about this weekend. I missed seeing you guys last weekend. I've gotten used to hanging out, it was weird."

"We felt the same, but we understood the reason behind it. We want you to be as safe as you can be. We know it's not always easy. I wish there was more we can do."

"You do more than you know," I whisper.

CHAPTER TWENTY-SIX

The Boys-Maximus

Finally, Saturday is here. This week took forever. But now, we get Callie all to ourselves, all day long. First stop is the mall, once Callie gets here, which should be any minute. This day is going to be awesome! I'm so glad we don't have to go to that horrid dance. I would have, if Callie had been going, but only for her. There is no way I could have gone with someone else. I know that, my wolf does too. Hell, he knew from the first scent of her. Vanilla and strawberries smell good, but on her, it makes her smell good enough to eat, or lick, I'm not picky. It's like thinking of her scent magically conjures it, because I just got a strong whiff. My wolf and I want to roll around in that scent all day. It takes a moment, but then I hear her laugh.

Ah, my angel is here. We are still trying to navigate this relationship with Callyn. All of us guys want to shout from the rooftops. It's killing me not telling her, and it kills me that we have to leave her in that house with her father. My protective instincts are riding me hard when it comes to that.

Callyn walks into the living room. I have to resist the urge to growl. She looks good enough to eat. She is wearing black skinny jeans, her black boots, long-sleeved red hooded shirt. She can be little red riding hood, and I'll be the big bad wolf. I'll huff, and I'll puff, but it won't be grandma I'll be eating. Good God man slow your roll. She looks amazing, combined with her scent, I just want to howl at the moon.

She looks over at me and smiles. "Hey, Max."

I'm up and out of my seat before I know what I'm doing, heading her way. I need to feel her against me. I have to go to her, looking like that. I'm standing in front her; I smile quickly before I scoop her up into a hug. Her arms go around my neck, with her legs dangling. But it's not close enough. Keeping one arm around her back, I move my other down to her leg. Gripping the back of her thigh, I move it slightly letting her know what I want. She understands, because in the next second she wraps her legs around my waist.

My arm wrapping back around her, pressing her so close not an inch of space is between us. I bury my face in her neck, taking a deep breath. I want to lick and nibble at her pulse point. Instead, I gently kiss that soft spot right behind her ear. I feel her body shudder.

"Maximus," she says in a breathy whisper.

Her hand tugging at the hair at the nape of my neck. She says my name, making it sound like a prayer. The sound of my name coming from her lips, like that, almost brings me to my knees. Callie pulls back enough to look me in my eyes. She bites her bottom lip, eyes sparkling. She's just as affected as I am.

My mate is absolutely beautiful. I want to kiss the shit out of her. I lean to do just that when someone clears their throat. It brings us out of our daze, out of the little bubble we are in. I would bet any money that Callie would let me kiss her, and I want to, so much. I don't think I've wanted anything more in my life. I can't wait to feel her lips against mine. It's only a matter of time. I bet when it happens, it'll be electric.

Callie unwraps herself from me, slowly sliding down the front of my body. Her eyes widen. Yeah, Angel, that's from you. I don't try to hide it, I want her to know just how much she affects me. I make sure she is steady on her feet before I let go and back up. I look over Callie's shoulder, seeing mixed emotions on the guy's faces. Thankfully, none are angry, because she belongs to all of us and we can't be jealous.

Callie takes a deep breath before turning and facing the others.

"You ready to go Callie?" Lucian asks.

"You could say that," she murmurs.

I don't think she meant for us to hear that, but since we are shifters and have exceptional hearing, we did. We all laugh. Her cheeks turn a rosy shade. I move closer and throw my arm around her shoulders, pulling her closer to my side. I kiss the side of her forehead.

"Let's go, Angel," before I do kiss you. I want to see the sparks fly.

Lucian

I can't be mad at Max. We all know that she belongs to all of us, but decided not to push her, to let her come to us on her own. He did what all of us have wanted to do and have thought about doing. It shouldn't be much longer now. The Council is bound to find something. I don't care what they say, they will not take my mate away from me. I don't care if they find out she is completely human. Fate made her our mate for a reason, I'm damn sure glad they did.

Callie doesn't realize it, but she always makes sure we get equal attention. We're walking around the mall and every so often, she'll switch holding hands with someone. She makes sure she engages all of us in the conversation. She is getting slightly attuned to our feelings, always making sure we are okay. I'm pretty sure she can even tell when we are not being quite truthful. Her eyes seem to stare right through you.

Callyn's giggle brings me out of my thoughts and I focus on her. She looks so beautiful. I love the spark of life in her eyes. Just once I would like to see her pull her hair up and not hide behind it.

"So, when are we getting lunch because I'm getting hungry," Max asks. The next second a rumble could be heard. We all look to Callyn, who bursts out laughing, which causes the rest of us to as well. "We should feed her before her stomach starts to eat itself."

👑 👑 👑 👑 👑

The mall is packed today. Max and Callie are in the middle of yet another round of giggles and laughter, when a group of guys walk by. One looks our way, running his eyes over us and then over Callie. He passes by, but then quickly does a double take. This time lingering on her longer than I like. I let out a little growl, narrowing my eyes.

Mine.

The guys hear me and look to see what is going on. They follow my line of sight, seeing the guy ogle Callyn. Three more low growls can be heard.

"You might want to think twice about that, if you know what's good for you." You can hear the venom in Graydon's voice. The guy puts his hands up.

"Sorry, man. Didn't know. I was just looking."

"Well, look somewhere else."

The guy nods and walks away. We all glare holes in his retreating back.

"What was that?" Callyn's question has us whipping our heads back in her direction.

"Um, he was checking you out," Zeke answers.

"So."

"So, we didn't like it." Ever so tactful Graydon. Callyn narrows her eyes at him. Uh oh.

"And what exactly did you think he was going to do with the four of you standing right here? Hmm? What gives you the right to dictate who I can, and cannot date? If I was interested in someone you wouldn't stop me."

Graydon takes a menacing step towards Callie. I tense, ready to spring into action if I need to. My eyes flicker between the two of them. I'm expecting Callie to back down, but she shocks me, by meeting him step for step. The toes of their shoes are touching. Graydon leans down, getting in her face.

"Like hell, I wouldn't. He isn't good enough for you."

"Oh, and you are? What are you going to do, chase away every guy that shows an interest in me?"

"Yes. We all are, and you're damn right; I'll make sure no one comes sniffing around what's mine."

Shit, I need to stop this, before he tells her something, we aren't ready to tell her. He might say something she's not ready to hear and deal with.

. . .

Graydon

Fuck, I might have just blown this. She just gets me so worked up. I just said she was mine. Damn, I'm so stupid. She's going to call me out on that, and what the hell am I going to say? She's not supposed to know. I just want to pull her into my arms and kiss the shit out of her. I want to make her forget about any other males, but me. I'm all...*we're* all she needs. My chest is heaving and I'm trying to control myself.

"We?" she questions.

I gesture around to the rest of the guys. "Yes, we."

She looks around to the other guys. A slow blush creeps along her cheeks, and damn if I don't want her more. I clench my fists at my sides to keep myself from reaching out to her. She takes one step back and then another, putting some space between us. She lets out a deep breath. My Callie bear is just as affected as I am.

"Come on guys, let's go get something to eat. The movie starts in two hours and we promised to take Callie to that diner in town," Lucian says.

Callie clears her throat. "You know what, that sounds like a great idea."

She moves forward and grabs Lucian's hand. As she walks by me, she gives my arm a quick squeeze, letting me know we're okay.

👑 👑 👑 👑 👑

We're sitting at a booth in the diner, watching Callie wolf down a chocolate strawberry cheesecake. There are two reasons why none of us have asked her for a bite: one, I'm afraid she might stab my hand with a fork. Two, the sounds...God the sounds she is making while eating the cheesecake would tempt anyone. They should be illegal. Callyn finally notices us all staring at her.

"What?" She looks at each of us.

We all shift uncomfortably in our seats. Zeke is running his hand over the back of his neck, while Lucian is trying to avoid eye contact. Max keeps running his hands through his hair, and I'm over here bouncing my knee like a kid hyped up on sugar.

"Must be some damn good cheesecake," states Max. Callyn blushes.

"Sorry, I should have asked if you guys wanted some, but when I had that first bite I couldn't help myself. It's sooo good. I've never had anything that tasted like that before."

"It's alright Callyn, we're glad you like it. Next time we'll get more than one. One piece wouldn't have been enough for all of us anyways." Lucian, always ready with the diplomatic answers. This is why he will make a good Elder on the Council, assuming there will still be a Council if the prophecy comes true, and Callyn and us are who we think we are. He places his hand over Callyn's, which has been fidgeting since she noticed us staring at her. She nods her head.

"Guys, the movie starts in a half an hour. I want to get good seats and snacks," Max says rubbing his hands together.

We pay and head out to Lucian's car. I hang back watching Callie joke around with guys. I feel like an ass about what happened earlier, and Callie really hasn't spoken to me since. I hate it. The same thing happens when we get in line to buy our tickets. I shove my hands into the pockets of my jeans. I am walking behind everyone, not paying attention to where I was going, my eyes cast to the floor. The next thing I know, I'm bumping into someone. I look to see it's Callie. I reach out to make sure she is steady on her feet.

"Sorry, Callie, I wasn't watching where I was going." I drop my hands.

"You okay?" she asks. I shrug my shoulders. "If it's about earlier, it's okay. I'm not mad."

"It seems like it. You haven't talked to me since. I know I was an ass and I shouldn't have said what I did. I'm sorry."

A smile spreads across her face. She holds out her hand and I take it. "How about you sit next to me inside? If you're nice I'll even share my snacks."

I laugh, as she starts to drag me toward the others. I didn't let go of her hand the whole time we were in the theater. I hold on like it's my lifeline because that's exactly what it is, what she is.

. . .

Zeke

This day couldn't have been more perfect. My only complaint is that we were getting ready to watch Callie leave and go home.

"I had a blast today guys. Seriously, this has been one of the best days I've had in a long time. It was nice getting away. Forgetting," Callie says.

This time it's me that gets up and hugs her. It's not the same as the hug she shared with Max earlier, but hell if it doesn't feel good to have her in my arms, to have her scent on me. She's so warm and soft and cuddly. Yeah, cuddly. It's getting harder every day to keep secrets from her. I hope that when we get to finally tell her everything, once we know everything, that she doesn't hate us.

"We'll do it again soon sweetheart; I promise."

I kiss the top of her head and take one big deep breath. Vanilla and strawberries never smelled so enticing before. I back up, feeling bereft without her in my arms. Callie sighs. I know she doesn't want to go home, but we don't have a choice. She grabs her bookbag that is by the door. We all walk her to the door, and she gives each of us a quick hug before she leaves. We wait until we can no longer see her.

I hate that she's walking home, but just in case her father is home, we don't want to cause any problems for Callie. Lucian closes the door and we all shuffle back into the living room.

"Does anyone know if there have been any updates on Callyn, with the Council. Have they been able to find anything more on her lineage?" I ask.

"No, Grandfather says that besides that one scroll that had her mother's maiden last name, that was it. It wasn't even her mother's name, just the last name. They are connecting that with her just because the last name is the same. I hope that it is her lineage, that way the Council can't keep her from us. The only problem is that record was nothing from this century."

"So, she might have some shifter in her DNA?"

Lucian nods his head. "Yes, she might."

"Doesn't explain why she hasn't shifted then. Can her blood be that diluted?" Graydon is in a better mood, all because Callyn noticed he was quieter than usual. I swear those two are going to be the death of everyone.

The tension between those two is off the charts. I know once we are given the okay, Graydon's going to be the first one to act on his instincts. I can't wait to see Callyn's reaction.

"I know. I'm confused by the whole thing. It's this big puzzle that we can't solve." Lucian loves puzzles, but not being able to help solve it is killing him. I can see it in his eyes. I bet if the Council allowed it he would have helped and probably found what we needed by now.

I'm not saying there is anything wrong with the Council, but they're all old. They move slow and we're all too impatient to wait on them.

"I hate keeping secrets from her. I mean I know why we are doing it, but it sucks," Max interjects.

We all nod. I know what happened earlier at the mall, wouldn't have if she knew that we are hers. We are made for her, and her for us. Don't get me wrong, I didn't like how long that guy was staring at Callyn, but I know she's mine. I've known since the first day of chemistry. I felt this pull toward her. I wonder if she feels the same, or if it's only us because we are shifters?

"I wonder what kind of shifter she will be or would be?" I question.

"I'm betting on some kind of cat. Kitten got claws when she wants. Plus, it would explain why Graydon and her fight like cats and dogs, even though he is a bear shifter," Max says laughing.

I try not to laugh, but I couldn't help it. All of us but Graydon is laughing, but I can see the smirk on his face.

He shrugs his shoulders. "You're probably right."

CHAPTER TWENTY-SEVEN

Callyn

I knew as soon as I walked in the door what was going to happen. My father was sitting in his chair with beer cans on the floor and coffee table. He started early today. The belt he uses to beat me with was also on the coffee table. I put my bookbag down. He knows. Oh god, he knows. How? I could have sworn I was careful.

"I've been waiting for you," he sneers. "I saw something interesting today when I was out getting my beer earlier. You know what that was? I saw you across the street coming out of the diner. Then I saw four boys follow you out. I watched for a minute. I saw all of you getting in the same car. All those after school activities you said you had, they were all just a cover, weren't they? You were out gallivanting around the town with those boys. Hm? You were acting like a little slut for the whole town to see."

He stands up and grabs the belt off the table. I take a couple of steps back. He is calm, but I know that is when he is the most dangerous. That's when the beatings are going to hurt more than normal. When my father is calm, all his anger will come out when he strikes with the belt. He walks over and is standing in front of me. I keep my head down hoping this will help. Oh, how wrong I am.

"I told you I won't have no slut living in my house. You've been meeting and fucking those boys, haven't you? You letting them all between your legs? Hmm?" he screams. He moves to stand behind me. "I hope spreading your legs was worth it."

I didn't even try to correct him. He won't listen to me anyways. The first hit of the belt is always the worst. The sound of the belt hitting my back echoes in the room. Without a pause in between, the belt hits just above the first hit. I try so hard to keep from screaming. Tears start streaming down my face. I lost count after the fifth hit. I couldn't take any more. I fall to my knees, but the hits just continue.

I curl into a ball, trying to make myself smaller. With every hit, I yell out. The back of my arms, legs, back, and butt get hit. I thought he would never stop. I hear the belt hit the ground and a few seconds later a door closes. I lay on the floor afraid to move at first. After a little while, I gather what little strength I have left and crawl to my bookbag. I grab my phone. It's finally time I did something. I can't keep doing this. Next time I might not be so lucky. I need help, but I can barely move. The pain is unbearable. I hit the screen and pull up the only numbers I have on my phone and hit the first name on the list.

Graydon.

After the second ring, he picks up.

"Hey, Callie bear."

I let out a sob. "Help me."

"Guys, we need to go now," he yells. The last thing I hear before I blackout is Graydon saying, "Hang on baby, we're coming."

CHAPTER TWENTY-EIGHT

The Boys- Graydon

My phone starts ringing. I look at the caller ID and smile when I see Callyn's name. Her dad must not be home because that's the only time she would risk calling. She wouldn't be afraid of being heard.

I answer, "Hey, Callie bear." I hear her whimper.

"Help me," she whispers.

My heart drops.

"Guys, we have to go now," I yell. "Hang on baby, we're coming."

I don't hang up; I want to hear in case something else happens. Plus, I need to keep Callyn on the line. I am checking my pockets for my keys when Zeke, Luke, and Max come rushing into the room.

"What's wrong?" Luke asks.

"It's Callyn. She's on the phone and something is wrong. She just asked for help. We have to go."

The look on their faces is shock, but every one of us runs out the door, and across the street toward my truck, it has the most space. I need Callyn to tell me what is happening.

"Sweetheart," she doesn't answer. "Callie bear," she still doesn't answer. "Callyn," I yell. Nothing. "No, no, no," she has to be okay. I look over at Zeke, "She's not answering."

"Go, Graydon. We need to get to her."

I nod, turn on the truck, and go as fast as I dare to get to Callyn's house. We don't even bother knocking. All of us rush in, I am floored by the sight of Callyn laying on the floor. I rush over to her; my hands are shaking. I place two fingers at the pulse point on her neck, I sigh in relief when I feel a steady rhythm beneath my fingers. I look to the others, who are all staring at me.

"She's breathing."

Lucian comes over and kneels beside her. He moves her hair from her face.

"Callyn, come on baby, open your big brown eyes. Please, baby," his voice barely a whisper.

Max and Zeke come over and kneel next to her. All our hands hovering over her, afraid to touch her. After a few moments, we hear a groan, everyone visibly relaxes. Her eyes flutter open.

"Luke?"

"I'm here baby," he says.

"So am I, Callie bear," I say.

"We're here too sweetheart," Zeke says.

She breaks down and starts sobbing and it guts me.

"Baby, can you tell me what's wrong? What happened? I'm afraid to move or touch you."

"He beat me, and it hurts so much," she says through the crying.

"Where baby?"

"My back hurts the most."

"Do you care if we look?" She shakes her head. Max, who is at her back, slowly moves her shirt up. Callyn lets out a whimper, the same time Max sucks in his breath.

"Oh, angel," he says. He looks up at us and you can see the tears welling up in his eyes. It must be bad. The rest of us shift to look. I gasp, you can see the old bruises in some areas, but the new ones are horrendous. Some are so bad that they've started to bleed. Her whole back is covered. We need to get her to the hospital.

"Baby, do you know why your father did this?"

She nods. I swear to all things holy that I will beat the fuck out of her father. How could anyone do this, especially to his own daughter? This beautiful, smart, wonderful, girl.

"Why, Callie bear," I say as soft as I can, as I try to control my anger. She clenches her eyes.

"He knows," she whispers.

"What does he know?"

"About you guys," she states as she starts crying even more.

"We need to get her to hospital. Once she gets looked at, we can figure this out," Zeke exclaims. Everyone nods and he moves closer. "I'm going to pick you up sweetheart."

All Callyn does is nod. He scoops her up and she lets out this ear-piercing scream before falling silent. My heart is breaking after hearing that sound. My bear is restless, wanting revenge for the harm done to our mate. I can't blame him; I want it too. I move closer to check on her; she's passed out. Zeke cradles her to his chest, as we all stand. I hear a door being opened from down the hall. A man stumbles out, clearly drunk, her father. I clench my fists, fighting every instinct to go and beat the shit out of him. My bear is roaring at me. He likes that idea. Her father deserves to get back everything he did to her, and more. This asshole touched my girl, hurt her, for years.

"So, you're the friends. What, is she screwing all of you? Are you the reason she is acting like a whore?" he slurs.

OH. HELL. NO.

Lucian

Graydon makes a move to go after Callyn's father but I grab onto his arms. He looks at me and I shake my head.

"I'm not going to stand here and listen to him talk to, and about her, like that," he growls.

"We're not. We're going to take Callyn to get the help she needs, and make sure she never has to set foot in this house again. Go help Zeke get her in the car. Max and I will make sure he doesn't come after her."

He lets out a ragged breath, letting me know how wound up he really is. Graydon looks back at her father before turning to me and nodding his head. He moves ahead of Zeke to grab the door.

I turn to look at her father. "If you ever come after her like that again, I won't stop him from coming after you. He won't be the only one," I said menacingly.

"You dare threaten me in my own home, boy?" He takes a step toward me and I take one towards him. I won't back down. He stops. He knows I'm not intimidated by him. I'm not a small, defenseless girl.

"Threaten? No. Warning? Yes. Unlike Callyn, you don't scare me. Lay one hand on me, my friends or her, and I promise it'll be the last thing you ever do." I gave Max a nod of my head to signal for us to leave.

When we approach the truck, we see Zeke and Graydon in the back-seat with Callyn laying across their laps. I take the driver side and Max the passenger. The keys are already in the ignition. I glance back and see her eyes are still closed. I don't know if that is a good or a bad thing. A part of me wants her to sleep so she doesn't feel the pain. The other part of me needs to see her eyes, to reassure her that she will be alright, and we will be there with her every step of the way.

Turning back, I start the truck and head to the hospital. I'm constantly looking in the rearview mirror to check on her. At one point, I see Graydon rubbing circles on her ankle and Zeke rubbing circles on her shoulder. I don't think they are even aware they are doing it. They are both staring out their windows, lost in their own thoughts.

This brave girl. We knew. She fucking told us! But she downplayed everything. Now, I'm wondering how many times he has done this to her over the last couple of months. Well, not anymore. No way my girl is going to go through this again.

The Council cannot let this continue. Human or not, Callyn could very well have lost her life. It doesn't matter that they abhor the fact that she is our mate, she is still a person. They must help now; there is no way they can let this continue. I won't, no we won't, let this continue. If I must stand up to the Council and my grandfather, I will face each and every one of them down. From this moment forward, I will protect my mate, no matter the cost.

Maximus

We are quiet on the drive to the hospital. That silence has extended to the waiting room. We all called our parents, to let them know what's going on, and all of them rushed here. So now all of our parents are here, waiting to hear any scrap of news on how Callyn is doing. It's been hours. I'm going out of my mind and I'm not the only one. Graydon keeps getting up and pacing. He'll do that until his father tells him to sit down, then a few minutes later he's up and doing it again. Lucian keeps running his hands through his hair, and Zeke is staring off into space, bouncing his knee. I keep running my hands down my thighs, not knowing what to do with my hands.

I can't take the silence anymore. "Guys." They all stop and look at me, even our parents. "What are we going to do? She can't go back there."

"First, we make sure she reports this to the police. I'm not letting that asshole get away with this," Graydon states.

"Graydon, you need to calm down," his father injects.

"I can't, not until I can see her. But I'm serious dad, he can't get away with this."

"I'm not saying he should. You are right, she needs to talk to the police. She must be the one to do it t. You can't force her," he says.

We all nod. "What are the chances of her having to go into foster care? She'll be eighteen in a few months. I don't know if I can take not seeing her anymore, I don't want her to leave. She can't leave, we just found her," Lucian says, his voice is thick with emotion.

"How about we worry about all this after we can see her. I don't care about that right now. I just need her to be okay. I need to see her eyes open. I need to hear her voice," Zeke growls.

We all fall quiet. I have to agree with him, I need all that so much. I didn't even know how much until then. My girl is lying in a hospital bed, who knows how broken. All I want to do is make sure I'm there to help her piece herself back together, I'll even use gorilla glue if I have to. I'll make sure she comes back better and stronger than before. I listen to what I'm saying. Holy shit, I like her. I mean I knew that, but it really just hit me exactly how much. I take a deep breath.

I can't...we can't hide our feelings about Callyn anymore. Not to each other, and especially not to Callyn. She has a long road ahead of her. She is going to need all the love and support she can get. I know three other guys willing to do whatever it takes to help her through this. By the looks of it, our families will be there helping us along the way.

Zeke

I can't believe I just said that shit out loud. I've been thinking about this for a while. If I'm honest, she had me hooked from that first day. My wolf, from the moment we smelled her scent. The man, not soon after. The more time we spent together, the more I started to like everything about her. She is kind, sweet, and sexy. I can sit for hours and listen to her talk. As every day passes, I fall a little more. Now, I'm sitting in a hospital waiting room trying not to break down, because I can't be back there with her.

My sweet Callyn. My brave, yet timid, girl. I hear a sound and see the doctor coming through the doors. All of us stand, but me and the guys move closer to the doctor.

"She's awake. A couple of you can go back and see her. I can't tell you anything about her injuries since none of you are her legal guardian. However, I can't stop her from telling you." We all nod. "I'll take a few of you back to her room. Who's coming?"

"I am," all four of us say at the same time.

"Alright, then. Follow me."

The doctor leads us down the hall and turns right. He stops at a door on the left, about halfway down the hall. "Now, she might be a little loopy. We gave her some medicine to help with the pain." He turns and walks away.

All of us just stand there looking at each other. I take a deep breath. Screw this I'm going in, they can follow or not, but I'm not waiting another second to see my girl. I push open the door. Callyn is laying on her side when we enter the room. I move over to her bedside and hear the shuffling of footsteps behind me. Graydon, Max, and Lucian come to stand around her bed. We basically form a protective wall. Good. We'll make sure nothing ever hurts her again.

"Callyn," I whisper. She moves slightly looking up meeting my eyes.

She quickly glances around and sees the rest of us are there too. Her eyes light up like a Christmas tree. The smile she gives us, almost brings me to my knees. I want to grab her face and kiss the shit out of her, and I know right there, I'm a goner. Stick a fork in me, I'm done. Callyn owns my heart and soul.

CHAPTER TWENTY-NINE

Callyn

"Callyn?" It was nothing more than a whisper, but I would know that voice anywhere. Zeke, my Zeke. I look up and meet his eyes. Those beautiful hazel eyes look at me like he can see into my soul. I look around and see that all my guys are here. I smile. Nothing has made me happier than seeing them. Lucian moves his hand, like he wants to touch me, but decides not to and pulls his hand back. I look at him, my brown eyes meeting his.

"It's okay Luke. I won't break."

"Oh, baby how can you say that? You're lying in a hospital bed. God knows how seriously you're hurt," he exclaims.

"Because Lucian, I'm still here. My father may have beaten me, and I may be bruised, bloody, and scarred, but I refuse to let him break me. I will heal from this. My spirit may be slightly broken, but I'm hoping to have you, all of you, to help me along the way."

"Like you could get rid of us," Graydon says.

"Yeah, we're not going away that easily. I'll even bring the glue to help piece you back together," Max says smiling.

I smile, "Good," I say as the tears start to well up in my eyes. I need them, all of them. They came for me and they helped me. Will help me.

"Why the tears sweetheart?" Zeke asks as he gently touches the side of my face.

"Because you care, and because you're here."

"There is nowhere we would rather be." He leans down and places a quick kiss to my forehead. "We were so worried. Still am, if I'm honest. Can you tell us what happened?"

I nod. I ask if they could help me sit up. Zeke is the closest, so he does. I sit without resting my back on anything. They all sit gingerly on the bed, not wanting to hurt me, each placing a hand on my legs. It feels nice to have them comfort me. I don't think I can get through this without each of them. I tell them how when I got home, my father was waiting for me. He saw us in town. I was supposed to be at the library, and I wasn't. Then he paid more attention and he realized I was with four guys; that set him off even more. I told them how he hit me. I started crying, reliving it again. They each start to rub a circle pattern on my legs, it helped me tell the rest of the story.

I called them the second he walked away. The doctor said my back is bad and that I will have some scars from where the belt cut me. It will take weeks for the bruising to fade. I have to clean the cuts, so they don't get infected. I have blood blisters everywhere. They are giving me some cream and muscle relaxers to help with the pain. There will also be some low dose pain reliever that I am to take only when needed.

My back will be tender for a while, and that he wouldn't suggest laying down on it. My back will probably get stiff, because the slightest movement will hurt for a few days, and it will make me not want to move, but I have too. When I get cleared to go back to school, I'm not allowed to carry my bookbag. Once the blisters, cuts, and the bruising start to fade, I'll be able to do everything normally. I am to take it easy, light-to-no lifting for a week. After that, I can do small things but nothing too strenuous.

I have a follow-up appointment in two weeks, to check the healing process. He gave me a number for a therapist he suggested that I call. The doctor said he was waiting for me to wake up, so that he could call the police. He asked if I wanted to press charges, and I told them I did. They all let out a sigh of relief. I can't live like this anymore. Who is to say that next time he won't go further. He could kill me. I'm probably lucky that he didn't already. I go to reach for the water cup on the stand next to my bed, but the twisting motion sends a radiating pain through my back. I suck in a breath. Max rushes over to help.

"I'll get it, next time just ask. We'll help you," Max says as he hands me the cup.

"Thank you." I take a sip. "When the cops do finally get here, I'm going to tell them everything, but I'm scared. I don't know what's going to happen to me."

"Whatever does happen, we are going to be here with you every step of the way," Lucian states. I look around me and see every one of my guys are nodding their heads in agreement.

I love them. I don't know if I could do this without them. I need them, all of them. I just didn't know how much until now. When my father was coming after me, they were the first thoughts I had. I had to get to them. I needed them to come and help, and they did. They came and rescued me. There is not one doubt in my mind that they will be here to help. I don't deserve them, but damn I'm going to be selfish.

There is a brief knock on the door before it opens. The doctor walks in with a couple of uniformed police officers.

"Sorry to interrupt, but the police are here to question Callyn."

"We'll be back when you're done. You got this Sweetheart," Zeke says before he kisses my forehead.

"Holler if you need us, Callie bear." Graydon leans down and kisses my forehead as well.

"Be strong, Angel," Max says right before he kisses my cheek.

"Just a little bit longer, Baby." Lucian bends down and kisses my other cheek. I watch as they all file out of my room. I square my shoulders as best as I can. I look at the police, preparing myself for what is to come.

I take a deep breath. You can do this Callyn.

You got this.

CHAPTER THIRTY

The Boys- Lucian

We all reluctantly leave Callyn's room, but she needs to do this. It's the first step to her healing. We all walk quietly back to the waiting room. Our parents look up. My grandma is the first to speak up.

"How is she?"

"Bruised, broken, scared, but she's hanging in there best she can."

"We saw the cops go back, I take that as a good sign and she's finally going to stop that monster?"

I nod my head. "Yeah, but I'm scared, Grammy." She gets up and comes over to me. She pulls me off to the side.

"What's wrong?"

"I just..., I just..." I don't know how to explain it.

"You love her, don't you?" she questions.

Did I love her? I think I might have fallen in love with her.

"I love her like I do the guys, as do my friends. But I think I might be Grammy. I might be in love with her."

"Love is scary Lucian." I shake my head.

"That's not why I'm scared." I glance up at the others, my eyes finding each of my friends. "What if she doesn't want any of us like we do her? What if she can't cope with being a mate to four guys? She is my destined mate, my one. What if she doesn't feel the same because she is human? What if I'm not enough or she doesn't want me as one of her mates? I hate not being able to tell her, but keeping secrets isn't going to help any of this, or anyone."

"Oh, Luke, you are enough. Do you hear me?" I nod. "Good. Now, I think this is a conversation you need to have with your friends. You guys need to come up with a solution, whatever that may be. But you don't push her into anything. Ultimately, this must be Callyn's decision. I will talk to your grandfather. The Council has stalled long enough. That girl in there could have lost her life. I will not stand by and let that happen; and I think you may be wrong about Callyn not wanting you. I believe she wants all of you just as much as you want her. She may not end up a shifter, but I believe she feels the effects like you do, just not to the same degree. I think it's about time you boys tell her who she is to you. I'll deal with your grandfather."

I nod my understanding. Grammy gives me a quick hug and goes back over to her seat. I look around and catch my friends' eyes. I let out a breath as they all walk over to me.

"You okay?" Max asks.

"Yes and no. But..., but I think it's time we talk. My grandmother thinks it's time to tell Callyn that she is our mate. She said she will help deal with the Council. She is not happy with the way things have turned out. But we do need to talk about how each of us feels about Callyn and the possibility that she may want one or none of us. She is human, and we don't know how well she will take this news."

This conversation should have already happened, but we were listening to the Council. I think it's about time that we stopped.

Graydon

No way in hell will I not give a fighting chance to be with Callyn. Did it cross my mind that she may not want any of us? No. But I must hold out hope that she does. I know that a relationship with four guys is unconventional to a human, but as shifters we understand. The question is, can we help Callyn understand? I know how I feel about her. How deep my emotions for her run. I think the guys need to confess theirs as well. Looks like I'm going to get the ball rolling.

"I'm falling in love with her. I want her and I think she wants me, possibly all of us," I state boldly. I was waiting for the yelling to start but it didn't. No one said anything. I look around meeting each of their eyes. Zeke was the first to break the silence.

"I agree with Graydon, with all of it."

"Me three," states Max.

"I do as well."

"I figured as much. Well, where the hell do we go from here?"

"I don't know, but now really isn't the time. We can talk later, when Callyn is resting. We also have to decide when we want to tell her," Lucian says.

I say we tell her as soon as we go back to her room, but logically, we should wait until she is feeling better. I just don't know how much longer we can wait.

👑👑👑👑👑

Another hour and a half go by before we see the police leave. Our parents left about an hour ago, making us promise to tell them the second something changes. Also, that we aren't supposed to stay here all night, and we are expected to come home. Like I'm going to listen. Callyn literally doesn't have anyone right now. I can't leave her here by herself. After everyone's confessions, I doubt they will leave either.

We watch the police stop and talk to her doctor for a moment, before turning and walking out the door. Callie's doctor walks over to us.

"Callyn has asked for you guys to return to her room when you can. Visiting hours are done at ten," he says sternly, before turning and walking away.

We all get up and start walking back to her room. I pause outside her door, turning to look at the guys. "We can't say anything to Callie yet. We don't even know what we are doing, let alone what she just went through. We have to give her time to heal. Agreed?" I say barely above a whisper.

I look each of them in the eyes and they all nod their heads in agreement. I turn back and knock on Callyn's door.

"Callie bear, it's us."

"Come on in."

We all file in and take up posts around her room. I look at her face and her eyes are red and puffy. She's been crying again. I clear my throat. God, I hate this.

"How are you holding up?" I ask.

"Best as can be expected, I guess."

"I hate to ask Callie bear but what did the police say."

I see her eyes well up with fresh tears, and I feel like an ass for asking, but I need to know. She lets out a deep breath.

"They are going to go and arrest him. I told them about my aunt. They said that they will try to locate and find her. If they can't before I'm released, I'm going to have to go to a group home. I don't want to, but I don't have a choice."

Callyn breaks down and starts crying. Lucian and I sit on one side of her bed, Zeke and Max on the other. All of us put a hand on her leg.

"When are they going to release you?" Lucian questions.

"The day after tomorrow. What if my father's not there when they go to arrest him? He has to know that the cops would be called."

We glance quickly at each other. Chances are that he is passed out drunk in his room. We didn't think about him trying to skip town. Someone should have stayed to make sure, but we didn't know if Callyn would tell the police. I send a quick message to my dad to see if someone can go to Callyn's and make sure everything goes well when the cops arrest her father. I send the address. A few seconds later, he lets me know that Lucian's grandmother already had it taken care of. Elder Harris is going to Callyn's to watch things. We were so worried about her that nothing else mattered. It still doesn't. Callie comes first and always will.

Zeke

An hour later, there is a knock on Callyn's door. Lucian's grandfather pokes his head in. "I need to speak with you boys for a moment." We file out of the room and into the hallway. "I figured it out," he says without missing a beat.

"Figured out what grandfather?"

"Callyn."

We all stand there waiting for him to say something. Instead, he reaches into the front pocket of his robes and pulls out a necklace. Letting the chain unravel, we see a pendant on the end. All of us move closer to take a look. It is a round silver pendant with a star in the middle. In the center of the star is a diamond. There is a black circle around the star. The symbol for air is at the top with an aquamarine diamond at the tip. Earth is at the bottom with an emerald, fire is to the left with a ruby, and water is to the right with a sapphire. Lucian inhales deeply.

"Is that what I think that is?" he questions.

"Yes."

Lucian quickly meets all our eyes. "This is the symbol of the Alpha Queen. It was mentioned she wore a necklace made of silver, on that necklace hung this symbol. It was said to be passed down to the next reigning queen. The last Alpha Queen never had an heir."

"That we know of. Remember, we don't know what happened the night she met her end. I do need to ask Callyn how she came by this though. I just need her to confirm my suspicions."

We nod, curious as to where he is going with this. We shuffle back into Callyn's room. Her eyes go wide when she spots Elder Harris. He moves and takes a seat on the edge of her bed.

"How are you doing, sweetie?"

"The best that can be expected."

"I came across something in your room. I'm sorry, first for going through your belongings, but I was curious to see if there was a clue to help us unravel the mystery of you. I saw the jewelry box hidden in the back of your closet. When I opened it, I found this." He shows her the necklace.

Callyn frowns. "That's my mother's necklace. She gave that to me before she died. Why? What's so special about it?"

"Before I tell you, did she say anything else about this necklace?" She nods her head.

"Yes. She said to never show anyone. When the time came, I was to pass it down to my first-born daughter. She said it has been passed down for generations and it's a very special and valuable heirloom."

"Do you know what this symbol is?"

"No."

"I do." Callyn lifts her head.

"It's the symbol of the Alpha Queen."

"Alpha Queen?"

"Yes. Callyn, what I'm about to tell you will come as a shock, but I need you to listen carefully. Then I will let the boys take over. There are things that are still unclear even to us, bear that in mind. This necklace is said to have been worn by the Alpha Queen, handed down to their heirs when it was their time to rule. The last known queen to have worn this was around two centuries ago. She and her mates were defeated in a great war. Everyone thought that she bore no children, thinking that when she perished, so did her line.

Now, I'm not so sure. This necklace may just prove that you, Callyn Silvers, is a descendant of the Alpha Queen. The true ruler of all shifter kind. These boys, all four of them, are your true destined mates. Thus, making you all the first true alpha pairing in two centuries. Which also means, you all have a lot of responsibilities, and work ahead of you. The only way you are going to get through this is together."

Maximus

Holy shit.

Could Elder Harris have dropped a bigger bombshell? Callyn being in possession of the Alpha Queen's necklace practically cemented what everyone thought. Thinking and knowing are two different things. I'm a mate of the Alpha Queen. I'm basically royalty. Hell yeah!

"Shifters are real?" Callyn questions.

"Yes. The boys are shifters. Practically everyone in this town is," Elder Harris answers.

"Okay, but I'm not a shifter. I mean, I don't have any other form besides this one." She gestures over her body, and what a body it is.

"That I don't have an answer to. It could be that your bloodline is now too diluted with human DNA and you can't shift. Another possibility could be, once you claim your mates it might awaken a dormant shifter gene. Only time will tell if you will be able to shift at all."

"If I could shift, what would I be? Could you explain about mates?"

"The Alpha Queen's line, the heir anyway, always shifted into a phoenix. Your mates are in this room. All four of these boys are yours."

"Aren't phoenixes like a myth? Mine? They are mine?" she gestures to all of us before a small smile appears across her lips.

"To humans yes, phoenixes are a myth, but not to shifters; and yes, they are yours."

Callyn may shift into a fucking phoenix! I don't know a person alive that has seen a phoenix shifter. It makes sense then if it's just royal blood that shifts into that mythical bird. Oh, man. I hope Callyn gets to shift, to see her spread her wings and fly. I bet nothing would look better.

"You know this sounds crazy, right? Shifters aren't real."

Elder Harris looks over his shoulder to Lucian. "Lucian, since your shifted form is smaller than the others, would you please do me the favor and shift for Callyn?"

He just nods. Lucian steps to the side, giving Callyn a full view. In a matter of seconds, the spot where Lucian was just occupying, now stood a red-haired fox. He moves to the side of Callyn's bed before jumping up. He has his head lowered, tail tucked between his legs, a sign of submission. The shock on my face must match that of Callyn's, but for very different reasons, hers from seeing a human turn into an animal, and mine because Lucian is submitting.

I look at the guys and see that they are just as shocked as I am. Lucian just submitted, to his queen, his mate. I look back to Callie. She lifts her hand tentatively. I can see her shaking from here. Slowly, she moves her hand toward Lucian. He lowers his belly to the bed and crawls slowly, meeting her palm with his nose before giving it a quick lick.

Callie giggles. "Can I touch you?" she asks him.

Lucian answers by crawling a little closer, nudging her hand with his snout. She places her hand on his head between his ears, before cautiously running her finger over his fur. In the quiet of the room, I hear a purr. What the hell Lucian? You're purring now too?

"Oh, your fur is so soft." Before I can blink, Callyn picks him up and starts to snuggle with him. "Oh my God, you're just the cutest thing," she says, as she rubs her face on the top of his head, and the side of his muzzle.

The purring gets louder. Lucky, fucking bastard!

CHAPTER THIRTY-ONE

Callyn

Listening to Elder Harris speak of shifters, being Queen, and having four mates was a bit much. Anyone listening would think he belongs in a looney bin! I didn't really believe him; I was just going along with it. Then I had to go and question him. He asked Lucian to shift. Then I thought I belonged in a looney bin. One minute, Lucian was standing there, handsome as ever. Then the next, there was a fox in the spot he was just standing.

The fox has the same red hair color as Lucian. When he jumps up on my bed, I almost scream. I look and see the fox had the same color eyes. This was Lucian. Holy shit, shifters are real. If shifters are real, then there is a possibility that everything else that was just said, was real too. I don't know if I can handle this. I want to touch him, but I am scared. So, I ask, and he lets me. He is just as soft as his fur looks. I couldn't help myself. I pick him up and snuggle him.

Oh God, this is going to be embarrassing later. Right now, he is curled up in my lap, purring, as I thread my fingers through his fur. I take a deep breath; I have a feeling that there is more. I want to know, but I also want to know what the other boys shift into, and I can't wait to see. I need to satisfy my curiosity first.

"What do the rest of you shift into?" I ask, looking around the room.

"I'm a wolf," answers Zeke.

"Me as well," states Max. I look over to Graydon, meeting his eyes.

"I'm a bear." I couldn't help it, I burst out laughing.

It takes me a minute to get control of myself. "So, you're telling me that I've been calling you my grumpy bear, and you quite literally are my grumpy bear." I start laughing again. The rest of the room joining in. It's a few moments before everyone quiets down.

"The guys had a good laugh about that, later that day."

I look back to Lucian's grandfather. "I sense that there is more."

"Unfortunately, yes. Before I continue, I would like to ask a question." I nod my head for him to go ahead. "Have you ever worn the necklace?"

"No. I was little when my mother gave it to me. She told me to keep it hidden and never show anyone. She said you never know who you can trust. So, I did as she asked. I never once took the necklace out of the jewelry box."

"Would you mind putting it on? I would like to see if anything happens."

"Okay," I say tentatively.

Elder Harris hands me the necklace, and I slip it over my head. At first, I didn't feel anything. But then the pendant starts to feel warm. A tingling sensation starts to spread over my body going outward from where the pendant laid on my chest. I gasp in surprise. It's weird, but I start to feel better. My back didn't hurt as bad. I look over at Graydon.

"Check my back."

"Why?"

"Please, just check it."

Graydon shrugs his shoulders, gets up and closes the few feet that separate us. I lean forward slightly, making sure not to press on Lucian, who was still curled up on my lap in fox form. I hear Graydon take a sharp breath in.

"It's healing right before my eyes! The bruising is fading, the blisters shrinking." He takes a couple of steps back, before the others walk over and look.

"Well shit, how?" whispers out Max.

"The necklace started to get warm and I felt tingly all over. I don't know, I just started to feel better, everything hurt less. But I don't understand," I say looking at Elder Harris.

"Magic, sweet girl. Magic."

AUTHOR NOTE

Firstly, I would like to say thank you for reading the first book in the 'Shifter Royalty

Trilogy'. I hope you enjoyed reading it, as much as I have writing it. If you made it this far, keep going. The playlist I listened to while writing 'Royals' follows. Also, there is a sneak peek at book 2, 'Queen's Guard'. I started writing this book during National Novel Writing Month, or NaNoWriMo, for short. The idea originally wasn't going to be about shifters, but I was almost done writing it when I felt it was missing something. The idea of having them be shifters came to me, and I loved the idea. I went back and rewrote most of the book to fit the new idea.

The cover is by Ampersand Book Covers. When I saw it, I knew. It just drew me in, and I knew I had to buy it. It also gave me the idea to make the main characters royalty. I hope you fall in love with the characters and their story like I did. I hope you will continue this journey with me and the characters, as they grow and learn what they are capable of. I hope to continue the journey and growth as a writer.

This is my first released book and I am nervous and excited at the same time. I have started and written so many books, but I never think they are good enough. The thought that no one would read them, also made me hesitate. I finally bit the bullet and hit the publish button, making my dreams come true. Thank you to all of you who have read and bought this book. It means more to me than you know, or I can express.

I would like to give a special thanks to my husband, for putting up with my ramblings and confusion about my book. For not really knowing what was going on, but still being encouraging and supportive. Thank you to everyone who I used as a sounding board and bounce ideas off. You guys are more valuable than you know. Thank you, everyone, and happy reading.

Much Love,
   S. Dalambakis

PLAYLIST

"Powerful"- Major Lazer, Ellie Goulding, Tarrus Riley
"Lights"- Ellie Goulding
"Grand Masquerade"- The Trouble Notes
"Dangerously"- Charlie Puth
"Tried To Tell You"- Brantley Gilbert
"Bad Girlfriend"- Theory of a Deadman
"Savin' Me"- Nickleback
"Dancing Without Me"- Shotgun Rider
"Defying Gravity"- Todrick Hall
"Digging My Own Grave"- Five Finger Death Punch
"Muddy Waters"- LP
"Living Dead Girl"- Rob Zombie
"Broken"- Seether and Amy Lee
"Devil's Backbone"- The Civil Wars
"Human"- Rag'n'Bone Man
"Light It Up"- Luke Bryan

SNEAK PEEK

Queen's Guard
Shifter Royalty Trilogy Book 2

Callyn

These boys, my boys, they know what they do to me when they touch me. It's been there from the very beginning, an energy drawing me to them. From the moment I first touched them I felt electricity run through my body. My energy, my magic is drawn to theirs, calling to theirs. Like now, with Graydon running his fingers down my arm. I can feel the tingle of magic lying under my skin. I know who they are, who they have always been.

Mine.

They're my mates and when they claim me, it's going to be powerful. Minute amounts of energy is released when we touch. It's been happening since we met, and we didn't know. It's part of the reason the Elder Council didn't want us together. They fear the power we will wield once we fully mate. We aren't ready for that just yet, but I want to see what their lips feel like. I want to see what happens. What kind of energy we could release. If Graydon doesn't stop, he's first on my list.

I peek at Graydon from the corner of my eye. He doesn't seem as affected as I do by him touching me. I bite my lip. What's stopping me honestly? He's mine. I can kiss him... them, anytime I want. Just go for it Callyn. I shift so that I'm sitting sideways on the couch. Graydon looks at me with a raised eyebrow. I bite my bottom lip again. The motion drawing his gaze. He shifts slightly, angling towards me. I lower my eyes to his perfect lips.

His fingers tracing the same path on my arm, but up instead of down. His fingers didn't stop, skimming my shoulder following the line of my collarbone to my neck. His hand expands around the base of my throat, not gripping. His hand slides up the slender column of my neck, stopping just under my chin. He tilts my head back slightly. My heart is pounding in my chest. Graydon searches my eyes. I try to convey how much I want... no, need this.

He curls his fingers under my chin, using his thumb to brush across my bottom lip. I part my lips, using my teeth to nip at the pad of his thumb. Graydon growls. He moves his hand to the back of my neck bringing me closer to him as he descends towards me. His lips crashing to mine. The second our lips touch, a jolt runs through me. It shocks me, causing me to part my lips, giving Graydon all the invitation he needs.

His tongue enters my mouth, tasting, teasing. I push my tongue into his mouth, doing the same. A burst of energy flows from us. Graydon growls, changing the angle of our kiss. My hands fist the front of his shirt, tugging him closer. Sensing what I was trying to do, he uses his free arm wrapping it around my waist. Keeping the hand on the back of my neck, he pulls me onto his lap. The motion causing me to straddle him. I let go of his shirt and press my body flush against his. My arms going around his neck, my hands fisting his hair, tugging slightly.

Graydon moans, pulling back just enough to look into my eyes. My chest is heaving, trying to get air. I know he can see the desire in my eyes, because it's reflected right back at me from his. His mouth finding my neck, kissing and nipping his way down. His teeth biting at the pulse point. I let out a moan before his mouth finds mine. Kissing me like I'm the very air he breathes. Devouring my mouth, like a man starved.

"Hey guys, did you feel that small energy wave. Oh."

I pull back to find Max standing at the threshold between the kitchen and the living room. I know I should be embarrassed, but I'm not. They're my mates. It's bound to happen. Then I go and do something unexpected, for me at least. I look Max in the eyes keeping the contact the whole time. I bend down and bite the pulse point on Graydon's neck. Max sharply inhales. I see his eyes sparkle. He likes what he sees. Graydon moans and pushes his hips up, his hard length meeting my core, eliciting a moan from me.

That's all it takes for Max to close the distance between us. I'm still straddling Graydon when Max's hands cup my face. Max crushes his lips to mine. He uses his tongue to coax my mouth open. I let him. The second our tongues touch, I feel another pulse of energy. Max moves his hands from my face but places them on my hips, lifting me off Graydon. On instinct my legs wrap around his waist, my arms going around his neck. I push myself as close to Max as I can get. We both moan. We change the angle of our heads, giving me a moment to draw in some much-needed air.

We kiss until we both need a breath. I look into Max's eyes. I love what I see there. Desire, longing, love. I give him the biggest smile I can muster. You can feel the spark. The current surrounding us. If this is how it feels to kiss these two, I shake my head. I can't wait to find out how kissing Zeke and Lucian will feel.

ABOUT THE AUTHOR

Hi! I am S. Dalambakis. I am a thirty-year-old mother of twins and a native Ohioan. I have been married for ten years, to a loving and supportive husband. I graduated from Youngstown State University, with a degree in Criminal Justice and Biology. I have been an aspiring writer for years and finally have the courage to release my writing to the world. I have a love for books and all things Harry Potter and "nerdy".

Come and stop by my Facebook page and Instagram.

https://www.facebook.com/s.dalambakis/
https://instagram.com/s.dalambakis

www.facebook.com/groups/Theroyalpack

Happy reading!

Made in the USA
Middletown, DE
23 February 2021